BANSHEES AND BLOODY MARYS

PARANORMAL COZY MYSTERY

MYSTIC ON THE ROCKS
BOOK THREE

LYNN M. STOUT

CHAPTER 1

"I guess we need to talk about last night," Connie said, her voice cutting through the cozy hum of the coffee maker.

As she refilled my mug, I couldn't help but sigh. Here we were, not even a day into what was supposed to be a ghost-free retreat and already we were trying to decipher the intentions of an irate spirit. The first evening of our quiet getaway was interrupted when we were wakened by a blood-curdling, in human scream.

Then came an equally blood-curdling human scream right outside the door to our condo. Connie and I rushed out of our bedrooms to find Lex on full alert standing on the back of the couch with his tail bristled and his back arched.

"Open the door. I'll check it out," he said.

As I flung the door open, a woman ran past.

"What's wrong?" I yelled.

"He's after me!"

I looked in the direction she came from. Nothing was there.

"Who?" I yelled after her disappearing back.

"The Captain," she said.

I looked again and this time I saw a floating figure at the end of the hallway. He wore what appeared to be a heavy pea coat with brass buttons. The man had a thick beard and wild, crazy hair that stood out all around his head. He had deep-set, dark eyes like black marbles. He moved down the hallway in a jerky motion, first appearing solid and then vanishing like a stop motion movie. He was fixated on the woman and ignored us as he passed.

Lex scooted past my legs and followed them.

"Should we go too?" Connie asked. "She might not be safe."

Before we could decide to follow, Lex returned and announced that the woman disappeared. Curious, we ventured into the hallway only to be met with the ghostly apparition.

Without warning, he appeared in front of us, staring with his dark, empty eyes. In a rather menacing way, he pointed to each of us before disappearing into thin air.

Lex, as usual, summed it up perfectly. "Creepy," he said. "Those black eyes. Yeah, guy is creepy."

I nodded and added, "Creepy, but not exactly violent, right? Sure, he seemed angry, but I didn't get the impression he wanted to harm us."

"Agreed," Connie said joining us with her own cup of coffee. "If he'd wanted to hurt us, he certainly could have. And think about all the spirits we've met who were simply unhappy with where they were and wanted to move on but couldn't. Even Vivienne was like that. After she died, she only wanted to move on peacefully. She didn't want to be with us any more than we wanted her with us."

"True. And considering how he was dressed, it's possible he had a violent death," I added. "Maybe he was a sailor who drowned. Plus, who knows how long he's been here?"

"Do your phone search thing," Lex suggested. "Can you find anything about the history of this place?"

We both tapped on our phones and after a few minutes, we had some general information. The ghost we'd seen last night seemed to be wearing what a ship's captain from the late 1800s would have worn.

"He must be a sailor from that time period," I said. "And remember, you yourself mentioned that the island was haunted when you booked the place. We shouldn't be surprised."

"I didn't really think it was, though," Connie groused. "I thought it was a tourist thing."

I think we all hoped the rumors of hauntings were just that, rumors. But after last night's encounter our hopes were dashed.

"Does it say anything about a shipwreck?" I asked peeking over her shoulder.

"Well, here it mentions that the lighthouse wasn't working and that there was a shipwreck, but then the article stops, and provides no details at all," she said.

"What do we do? I thought everything was online. How do you find out things if it's not on the web?" Lex's voice cracked.

Connie and I smiled. As bad and tough as he wanted us to believe he was, our daemon in the form of a cat, was instead a naive and lovable guy. He was brave and smart though and indispensable.

As Connie ran a comforting hand down his long back, I waved my hand to get their attention.

"There's a local historical society here. They have records, artifacts, relics...basically a potential goldmine! I think that's where we should start. You know, if we are really going to jump into this."

"I don't see how we can ignore it," Connie said. "We have an actual ghost running up and down our hallway. Plus there's the other thing that none of us is talking about."

Lex cleared this throat and jumped from the table. We both knew what she referred to. The inhuman scream that came just before the human one. Before we left, Tawny warned us that this island was known to have a banshee who wailed before someone died. I think all of us were wondering if that is what we heard, and if so, did someone die last night? No one wanted to say it out loud, though. I, for one, was more comfortable dealing with the Captain's ghost than with whatever that was.

Still, we found ourselves back in familiar waters, with a mystery to solve and a ghost to appease. At least this time it wasn't in our actual home and we could leave whenever we wanted to if it became too dangerous.

Not that we would. We were becoming pretty good at this, solving the unfinished business of ghosts who came to us while keeping our ability to see and communicate with them a secret from the living. Also, no one else knew about my telepathy abilities, yet I used them frequently. And we certainly weren't going to spill the beans about Lex. He could act like an actual cat when he needed to.

With mutual agreement, we decided to visit the historical society that very morning and start getting some answers.

CHAPTER 2

It was a short walk on a beautiful day along the east coast of Michigan. We meandered through the dappled sunlight along a well-worn dirt path. It wound through tall trees that bore the scars of multiple winter storms near the island's water. The leaves on the Aspen trees above trembled and flashed in the slight breeze.

As we approached the building that housed the museum, we slowed down. Connie and I went through the usual routine with Lex.

"No matter what happens, no matter what you hear or think, you absolutely cannot talk," Connie said.

Lex rolled his eyes. "This is getting old. I know the drill."

"Yet you consistently and continually ignore it!" I reminded him. "And that whole thing where you say the word 'me-ow' isn't fooling anyone. That's going to get you in trouble for sure."

"Well, it hasn't yet," he pouted. "You two go on. I'll take care of myself and do my own research, if it makes you feel better." And with that he scampered off, disappearing into the brush along the side of the small squat building.

Connie and I shared a look and went on.

"So we don't say anything about our ghost, correct? We simply ask some general questions."

"Yes, I think that sounds good. And we'll see how it goes before we say anything about that ungodly screech too. We can't be the only ones who heard it."

With our plan in place, we pushed open the door to the historical society and were met with a small mob.

A woman stood at the front of the room. She was very short, around five feet and wore capris with tennis shoes. She had her short hair pushed behind her ears and her glasses sat on top of her head. She was sweating.

"You know as well as I do there's nothing to be done. Sometimes the sound doesn't mean anything. You are overreacting and besides, what do you expect me to do about it?"

"Nora, you know better than any of us. People are dying. There needs to be an investigation!"

"Yes! We need answers!"

As the group became more vocal, an elderly man who stood to the side of the room cleared his throat. At the sound, the small mob grew quiet and the woman at the front spoke.

"Why don't you do it, Clem? You go talk to the sheriff and tell him what you need. He'll listen to you."

"Well, we all know that won't work, don't we?" A man in his late forties interrupted before Clem could answer. He was leaning against the counter next to the woman they called Nora. "We don't need to bother him. It never amounts to anything. Let's keep this to ourselves and -,"

"Mayor Alistair is right!" Another man interrupted. "What difference has it ever made?"

"This place is haunted and there's nothing we can do about it." A young woman with a small child exclaimed. Everyone in the room seemed to agree with her.

The mayor attempted a weak protest that the island wasn't haunted. No one was listening and he turned to Nora.

"Ask her!" He said. "Nora understands what's going on."

She turned to him with her mouth open. "Are you serious? I don't know anything!" Nora said, throwing her hands up. "I'm a volunteer! I don't have any authority. I don't mean to be rude, but please, go home and leave me alone."

As she said this, Clem approached her and put a comforting hand on her arm. He whispered something to her and she nodded.

"Look, everyone. It's been a long time since anything bad has happened and honestly, when someone has died, it's been from a disease or an accident. Remember Mildred Rascan? She had a heart attack. And Carson Stewart, remember him? He was driving drunk and ran off the road."

"What about all them that jumped from the lighthouse?" A man in the back yelled out. "Explain that."

Nora looked at Clem who shrugged his shoulders. Several in the crowd grumbled.

"I can't explain it any better than you can. I don't know any more than you do and I don't know why you think differently. Please go home."

Mayor Alistair smiled smugly at Nora then addressed the crowd. "Alright everyone, you heard Nora. She says she doesn't know anything. Go on home now." And she flapped his hands shooing them away.

The crowd turned and began making their way towards the door where Connie and I stood. We stepped to the side and allowed them pass. We overhead someone comment that we were strangers. While another wondered in a loud whisper if the rumors were making their way off of the island.

She raised her voice, "Mayor Alistair, mainlanders are coming now and ghost-hunting. That's not the kind of tourism we need around here."

Mayor Alistair nodded to her and waved while her friend agreed heartily. They both shot us a rather unfriendly look as they passed.

Little did they realize ghost hunting was absolutely the last thing we wanted to do.

"I guess we came to the right place," I whispered to Connie.

"Yeah, but I'm afraid to ask anything," she answered in a hushed tone. "Let's wait until everyone leaves. Hopefully, Nora will talk to us privately."

The mayor nodded curtly towards us as he left, followed by Nora with her arm looped through Clem's. They had their heads bent together and seemed deep in conversation as they paused outside the museum.

We didn't want to interrupt so while we waited for her to return, we busied ourselves looking at some of the artifacts and history from the previous century. The original lighthouse had been built in the 1880's during the time when the lumber industry was taking off in Michigan. In addition, as we had already learned, the Great Lakes were critical for transportation for not only lumber, but also iron.

"This was almost one hundred and fifty years

ago," I added. "So it would make sense that there could have been a shipwreck, right? This was before navigation was modernized and they relied heavily on the lighthouses."

"And from that little bit we read, something was wrong with this lighthouse. Maybe that's what caused the shipwreck that made our -,"

I poked Connie in the side. She stopped talking just before she said, "Captain become a ghost."

"Nothing was wrong with the lighthouse, rather it was the keeper who wasn't himself that night."

I'd seen Nora approaching and now she stood beside us.

"Sorry, I didn't mean to eaves drop but couldn't help overhearing. And it's obvious you are visitors here so it's sort of my job to help you out with the history of the place. I'm Nora, the curator and one of the historians on the island."

We introduced ourselves and engaged in small talk for a few moments.

"I have to apologize for the scene you experienced. People get upset about things and for some reason, they think since I run this place I have information that I'm not sharing with them. I don't, though. I share everything I find out. Unlike some people."

I wanted to know who the 'some people' were

that she talked about, but Connie was ready to get down to business.

"We have a lot of questions," she said. "Can you tell us about any shipwrecks? Who died? Who survived?"

I guess my questions would have to wait.

CHAPTER 3

Nora's eyes lit up. We'd obviously tapped into her area of passion and she excitedly began leading us around the little museum.

"This is the one I've studied the most. The ship was called the Mystic Mariner," she said. "She was considered a mid-sized cargo ship, made of sturdy wood. She had three masts and could carry heavy loads without needing deep ports. She carried iron ore, timber and other agricultural goods extensively across Lake Huron and relied on the wind rather than burning coal."

She pointed to a photo next to a drawing. Both hung on the wall.

"You can see here that the deck was open and the cargo holds were below, see the hatches? The ship's cabins and the pilot house were here, in the stern. You can't tell from the photo, but the captain's notes tell us the masts were painted bright yellow."

"Really?" I said. "Yellow? Why?"

"It helped identify the ship to other ships in the area. They all knew the Mystic had bright yellow masts. Even at night, they would light kerosene lamps on the deck and the glow was enough to show the yellow masts, as well as her name on the bow, to other vessels."

"Who's this?" Connie asked, pointing to a very old and tattered photo.

"That's my great, great grandfather, Captain Elias Thorne, the captain of the Mystic Mariner."

Nora's pride in her family and in her legacy was evident as she looked lovingly at the photo.

"Unfortunately, he died when my great grandfather was a baby. In fact, he died when the Mystic wrecked right here, off the coast. Despite having a flat-bottomed midsection, she still ran into rocks when she came too close to shore. It was a terribly stormy night. There's documentation of what that storm did to the island as well."

"That must have been before the lighthouse, then?" I asked. "For the Mystic to have gotten that close to shore?"

"Sadly, no. This is what I meant when I said the wreck wasn't the fault of the lighthouse, but rather the neglect of the keeper. Silas Hawking, was drunk and passed out so he didn't light the lamp that night."

Nora abruptly turned away from us and pretended to busy herself with a stack of papers.

Is that it?

I heard Connie in my mind and shrugged. That couldn't be it. We needed so much more information. But the fact that her great, great grandfather died needlessly, while tragic, was ancient history. Why was she getting so choked up?

We needed her to keep talking since she was our only source of information. It was obvious she knew much more than what was on the website. I tried to change the subject to something less emotional.

"How did the light in a lighthouse work? The lamp, and then what? Mirrors or something?"

That worked and Nora turned back to us, her eyes shining again.

"Yes, sort of. It had a Fresnel lens. They were made using a lot of little glass prisms and lenses arranged in a circle inside a metal frame. That way they would capture and refract the light from the lamp in the center. Then it rotated so the focused beam would sweep around in a pattern. This is the signal that the mariners used to identify the lighthouses. Each lighthouse had its own pattern."

"So if someone didn't keep the lamp lit, the whole thing would stop working?" Connie asked.

Nora nodded.

"They relied on both, the lamp and the Fresnel lens. Of course, the lamp being maintained and filled with oil had to be done by a person. In this case, it was a lazy, drunk person and the entire crew of the Mystic died that night. Once the masts snapped she would have gone down quickly considering what she carried. She was heavy. There are still remnants of the cargo at the bottom of the lake, even today. And here is a little bit of what's left of her."

Nora held a splintered chunk of wood in her hands.

"We are so sorry about this, Nora. Still it is a fascinating bit of history and we appreciate you sharing it with us," Connie said. "It means a lot. Your dedication is obvious."

I smiled and nodded along, gesturing towards the area where the crowd had been that very morning. This was my opportunity to ask who she was referring to earlier when she said "some people" didn't share information. But again, my question would go unasked and unanswered because Nora admitted something so surprising it made me forget.

"Yes, so you're wondering about that screeching sound you heard last night? This isn't something we normally share with visitors, sort of our dirty little secret here on the island, but since you saw the crowd, you already know more than most. We have a banshee here. She wails when someone is about to die."

CHAPTER 4

"Well, that went well," I commented as we picked our way back towards the hotel.

"I certainly didn't expect that," Connie agreed. "I mean, I appreciate her honesty and all, but I never expected she'd just lay it out there like that. 'Oh, sure, that's our banshee,'" Connie said using air quotes for her interpretation of Nora. "What do you think? It's all folklore and superstition, right?"

I laughed. "Okay, first off, you know better. Folklore? Superstition? Like living with ghosts and talking cats running around is folklore and superstition?"

"Not a cat. Daemon."

Lex had crept up behind us.

"Sorry, talking daemons who look like cats. Is that better?" I asked, throwing a look over my shoulder.

When I did, I noticed Mayor Alistair walking behind us. When he saw me turn around, he jumped behind a tree.

I lowered my voice. "I think we are being followed, and not at all discretely, by the mayor. He ducked behind a tree when I glanced back."

"On it," Lex said and disappeared into the bushes. The last we saw was a flash of grey and white. A few seconds later, we heard a man's scream and turned in time to watch the mayor leap from the woods, stumble and land on his bottom in the middle of the path.

Connie and I rushed over to make sure he was okay. By the time we reached him, Lex was sitting on his lap, trying to purr and act like a cat while at the same time, preventing him from standing.

"Mayor Alistair, right?" I asked extending my hand to help him up and nudging Lex out of the way.

"Yes, yes. That's right. I don't know who this belongs to," he waved a disgusted hand towards Lex. "I've never seen this cat before and it attacked me when I, uh, well, I was stopped here."

"Right," Connie said.

"I wasn't following you," he added even though we hadn't asked. "Just walking on the same path going the same direction. It's a small island."

By now Lex had wondered off again and after confirming that he was okay, we said an awkward goodbye to the mayor. We continued towards our hotel while the mayor turned back the way he had come, then seeming to think better of it, he pivoted back towards us.

"I was going this way, wasn't I?" He laughed at himself. "And where were you ladies going?"

"We thought we'd check out the lighthouse," Connie said. "Nora gave us some wonderful history about the island and the lighthouse so we are exploring."

"Ah, well. As luck would have it, I am also going to the lighthouse. Let me walk with you. I am considered the current lighthouse keeper, of course it's an honorary title since the lighthouse no longer works."

He was definitely a smooth talker, despite the fact that only a few minutes ago he was caught trying to follow us. And was taken down by a twenty-two pound tuxedo grey cat.

"I'm afraid you have the advantage here. You already know that I am the mayor of this island town, Mayor Eli Alistair at your service. And you are?"

Connie and I introduced ourselves and we all shook hands. We made small talk as we picked our way along the narrow dirt path, through the towering white pines and red oaks and the Aspen leaves continued their dance. The air smelled musty and damp and we could smell evergreens mixed in with the rest of the scents.

Occasionally a chipmunk would skitter across the path and while I doubted Mayor Alistair noticed, we could see the flash of Lex's grey tail chasing them through the underbrush. A stand of white cedars rose in front of us and then we heard the sound of waves crashing on the beach.

CHAPTER 5

"I'm still surprised that the lakes produce waves. Being from the south, our lakes aren't this big, of course, we only get waves like this from the oceans," Connie noted.

Although Charleston certainly has its share of battering from storms, this was different for both of us. Mayor Alistair explained a little bit.

"Waves here can reach six feet or even higher. And during storms, gosh, they can go as high as twenty feet. It's the wind coming in from the west and northwest, that make the waves hit at an angle. That adds to the rocky shoreline you can see there." He pointed into the distance.

"Is that where the Mystic Mariner shipwreck occurred?" I asked.

Mayor Alistair turned pale and shook his head.

"Nora told you about that I'm sure. She's

become quite fixated on it all. I'm convinced she knows more than she's telling. I'm sure she told you, we used to be engaged. But between you and me, her obsession with this entire thing was just too much for me. I have aspirations. In fact, I am slated to run for governor next election. Did she tell you that too?"

"Well, no, she didn't tell us any of that," I said. "And governor, huh? Do you think you can win that race? The current governor is very popular and has done an amazing job with this state."

"Of course, I can win. And it doesn't surprise me that Nora didn't say anything. She's likely still hurt that I broke it off. She's not quite the governor's wife type of person."

"Well...," Connie began.

I cut her off before she said anything else.

"What do you think of the banshee?" I asked.

Mayor Alistair was holding the door to the lighthouse open for us and when Connie asked, he let the door close in our faces.

"Now why would you ruin a nice conversation with talk like that? You look like intelligent, educated women. Why talk of superstitions and other 'woo woo' things? There's enough people on this island living like we're haunted or something. Don't get me wrong, ghost hunters are always welcome here, or at least their money is, but they won't find anything. Mark my words. And look at the time." He glanced at his wrist where I noticed there was no watch. "I've got to run. Help yourself to the information inside and maybe I'll run into you again soon. Enjoy your stay!" And with that, he was gone.

CHAPTER 6

Indeed, we did help ourselves to the information in the lighthouse. There were even more historical facts and many pictures that we both found fascinating.

The lighthouse was built out of local stone. It originally stood about one hundred feet tall, but through the years and the weather, and despite its very wide base, it was settling and was now just under one hundred feet.

We were standing in what used to be the keeper's quarters but had since been restored to make room for the museum and welcome area.

I hoped to see the Fresnel lens but instead had to settle for pictures of the original and then modern photos and drawings. The original lens suffered damage in one of the historic storms in the area and after it was removed, the lighthouse was decommissioned.

Still, we were able to climb the stairs and stand on the gallery deck. Thankfully the view was majestic. We needed some sort of reward for the arduous climb. Not even halfway up my knees were creaking, and Connie was rubbing her hip.

Out of breath and in need of ibuprofen, we could see the entire island. Connie commented, "We keep calling it an island, but it's really not. Have you noticed?"

"Yeah, everyone seems to do that. But there wasn't a bridge to get here. It does have an island vibe to it, that could be why."

"Yeah, and that one little strip of road probably floods when it storms. I'll bet it's an island."

I agreed. "Anything else to look at while we're up here?" I asked.

Connie shook her head. "I think I'm ready for lunch. What do you think? There was that little place a short distance from the hotel. Sandwiches and salads sound good?"

I agreed and added that a bottle of wine might be nice as well. "Since we are supposed to be on vacation."

Lex appeared at the top of the lighthouse. I noticed he was also a little out of breath but would never admit it.

"I'll bet anything this is going to turn into a

whatdoyacallit? A working vacation? Like where you're in a different place and all but basically doing the same thing you do when you're at home. Because you two can't let it be, can you?" He asked in between deep breaths.

"What are you talking about?" Connie asked, feigning innocence.

"The banshee, of course," he said. "And the ghost in the hallway last night. Did you discover any information about him?"

"No, we didn't even ask, honestly," I said as we started down the stairs. "Nora was so forthcoming about the banshee though, I'll bet she would be receptive to hearing about the ghost in the hotel, and she might even try to help us find out who he is."

"Not the mayor though," Connie added. "He's not going to be any help at all."

"I agree. There was something about him. He was holding something back. I could feel it."

"Any idea of what it was? Could you read his mind?" Connie asked.

"No, it's not working quite like that. It's easy for you and me, we already have a connection. Same with Lex. With a stranger though, I have to work a little harder and if they are actively hiding something, it's even more difficult. I know something is there. He's hiding something, lying about something, but I can't figure out what."

We reached the bottom of the lighthouse and felt a gust of wind hit as the main door closed.

"Was someone in here when you came up?" Connie asked Lex.

He shook his head. "No, but someone just left. Do you think they heard us?"

"I don't think so. We weren't that loud," she replied.

We continued in silence for a few minutes each of us revisiting our conversation and wondering who anyone who might have overheard us was thinking. Still, it was too late to worry about it now, and when we came to a little restaurant that sat at the edge of the pier, both of our stomachs rumbled.

Lex scampered off through the underbrush, chasing fox squirrels and we placed our orders. We settled at an out of the way table for two and began our lunch of sandwiches, French fries, and Chardonnay.

"I think we need to figure out who the sailor ghost is next," Connie said out of the blue.

"Okay, sure. That makes sense," I agreed.

"There's a connection there, don't you think?" She asked.

I nodded and cut my eyes to the side. "Don't look now but I think your connection just walked into the restaurant."

Of course she immediately looked.

Nora was at the counter ordering her lunch. She'd seen us in the corner and appeared to be torn between acknowledging us and ignoring us. I decided to make it easy for her and waved as I called her name.

"Nora! Hi! Come join us!"

She looked sheepishly around the cafe and shrugged as if to ask, "What could go wrong?"

We pulled an extra chair to our little two-top and she settled in.

"Wine?" Connie asked.

"No, thanks. Middle of the work day for me." Then she seemed to rethink her statement and changed her mind. "You know, a glass would be lovely. A nice change. And it's not like I'm doing brain surgery."

We laughed at the joke and Connie gave her a healthy pour of wine.

We made small talk for a few minutes, but I couldn't take it any longer.

"Nora, something seems a bit strange here. Can you tell us more about Mayor Alistair? He was following us when we left the historical society building and was trying to hide from us. Then when we caught him, he offered to show us around the lighthouse and tell us about it. When we mentioned the shipwreck that your ancestor was in, he got very weird and couldn't get away fast enough."

"And he mentioned you two used to be engaged? That's surprising. I mean, we like you," Connie said, then laughed when she realized what she'd said.

Nora laughed as well. "Yes, that was old news. It wasn't a very long engagement and the breakup was mutual, although Eli will never admit to that. He's sort of an ass," she looked furtively around the mostly empty cafe and whispered.

"There is more. A lot more and I'm happy to tell you everything I know, but not here. Some people are very touchy about the subject, and since he is the mayor, he has a lot of clout, at least here on the island. It's hard enough keeping the museum open without him being angry with me. Let's finish eating and go back to the museum. Then I'll tell you everything."

While we gathered our things and prepared to leave, Nora went back to the counter and spoke to the lady at the register. We didn't know what she was doing but wanted to give her space. She had information, we knew that much and whatever she was working on, we didn't want to interrupt.

CHAPTER 7

The walk back to the museum was strange. We all felt as though eyes were watching us the entire time. Connie and I thought Lex was creeping around and the strange vibe was coming from him. We discussed it through telepathy so as not to alarm Nora. She was being a terrific sport but as we'd learned over and over again, a talking cat was something that tended to drive a person over the edge.

Lex himself put our minds not so much at ease, when he announced that he was indeed following us, but only because he also had a strange feeling.

Something is out here, you guys. Please be careful.

Is it the Mayor again? I asked.

No, I don't think so. This is different. Not human.

And with that, our very not human daemon cat

closed down communications. We knew he was there. The random fluttering of birds and the frantic scampering of small rodents told us he was on the prowl. But as he chased them, something else was chasing us.

Finally, we made it back to the museum. Nora opened the door and closed it behind us with a bang.

"Sorry," she said as we all jumped. "It was strange out there. Like something following us. I hope that's not a bad sign."

"Nora, earlier today you speak so casually of the banshee. Yet the Mayor was so dismissive. And the people in town seem to almost blame you for her. What's the story? If you don't mind."

"I don't mind at all," she said. She checked that the front door was locked and put the 'closed' sign out. Then she winked and said, "Follow me."

We went through a nondescript door in the back of the museum and emerged in a library of sorts. While everything in the front room was clean and tidy, shiny and organized, this room was obviously a room where hard work was done. There were maps and other papers strewn about. Notebooks and pens scattered everywhere. Old photographs littered one table and some of them were matched up with drawings. It smelled like an old library, deep into the stacks. The room had that comfortable, musty old book smell that promises amazing adventures are coming.

A large couch with a low table sat along the wall. Nora motioned for us to sit. She smiled as she pulled another bottle of Chardonnay out of her bag.

"Ta-da!" She sang. "You are a terrible influence on me!" She laughed as she poured.

"If you can't set a good example, at least serve as a terrible warning," I laughed but my joke fell as flat as Nora's face did.

"I'm sorry. I didn't mean anything...," I tried to explain.

"No, it's not that. Okay. I need to know a few things before we start talking. First, why are you so interested in the history of this place? I mean, a lot of tourists are interested and come for the museums, but very few ask the questions you two are asking. And even fewer travel with their cat who they allow to roam the island without a care."

That caught us by surprise. "How did you find out about Lex?" Connie asked.

"I'm more observant than the normal person, I guess. Just as you keep asking me about these things and saying there's more to it, I feel the same. What is your story?"

"Well," I shot a look at Connie. She nodded slightly. "We also have some unique observational skills, I guess you'd say. Unusual things tend to happen to us. Like your banshee. We heard her the first night we were here. And the way the town reacted to her and how you tried to calm everyone. It all seemed very strange to us and we can sense that there's more to it. Also Mayor Alistair is absolutely hiding something. Of that, there is no doubt."

Nora nodded. "You are correct about that. He is hiding a lot of things. But first, your cat is sitting in the window behind you. I think he's trying to get your attention."

We turned to see Lex in a cartoon pose, three paws balancing precariously on the ledge, one raised as though he were waving. The side of his face was pressed against the glass and his eyes were huge and unblinking, looking sideways at us. His attempt to look innocent only made him look more guilty.

I swear he shrugged then said, "Me-ow."

Nora clapped her hands and laughed. "He's very smart, isn't he? Let's let him in. I love cats."

Before we could stop her, she opened the window and Lex tumbled into the room.

Don't talk!

I commanded.

Wasn't gonna.

He retorted.

"Can I hold him?" Nora asked.

Before we could answer, Lex jumped onto her

chair and waited for her to sit back down. Then he curled onto her lap. As she scratched his head and ears, she visibly relaxed.

Between a cozy cat faking sleep on her lap and a third glass of wine in the middle of the day, Nora easily spilled the beans.

"There are rumors, in fact, it's more than a rumor, that Mayor Alistair has journals written by the previous lighthouse keepers. He refuses to share them though. He always says it's because of a code or something stupid like that and the journals are personal and private, only for the eyes of other lighthouse keepers. Which is ridiculous. He calls himself the keeper, but he doesn't do anything except unlock the museum in the morning and lock it back at night. It's not like the lighthouse works or that ships even need it nowadays with the technology they've got. Still, he has some major history, handwritten by the ones who were there, and he refuses to share it with either museum."

"Why do you think that is?" I asked. This definitely went along with the feelings I had earlier from him. He was hiding something. He was the one keeping secrets.

"I don't know. And his dismissiveness about the banshee doesn't help. He hears her just as well as the rest of us do. Yet he will say it was an owl or some other type of bird, and then blame me for her. But, you heard her, didn't you? Do you think that was an owl?"

"No, it most certainly was not," Connie said. "I've heard owls before. That sound woke me from a dead sleep and sent shivers down my spine. Well, that and what we saw afterwards."

I cleared my throat and Connie stopped talking.

"Now, see? That's what I was talking about. There is something else you aren't telling me. That you'd stop in the middle of a thought like that. What is it? Come on. I live on an island with a screeching banshee, I can handle whatever it was you saw."

Once again, I looked to Connie. She shrugged slightly and nodded her head.

"We saw a ghost, Nora. It looked like a sailor from a long time ago. He had a large, bushy beard, wore an old pea coat with brass buttons, boots. He seemed angry and a little scary. We tried to follow him because he was chasing a woman down our hallway. But we couldn't find the woman or him. We wondered if he's related to the banshee somehow?"

Nora nodded as we spoke. She didn't seem concerned or alarmed. Mostly curious and intro-spective.

"I've heard rumors of that. Whisperings from other tourists who stayed at that hotel. Of course, no one who lives here ever experienced it. Since we live here we don't stay in the hotel. So I guess I've always chalked it up to overactive imaginations. They learn about the banshee, and maybe even hear her, and now they are seeing ghosts in the hallway." She chuckled to herself and took a long sip of the wine. "But come to think of it, the descriptions are usually the same. They kind of remind me of my great, great grandfather. I showed you his picture, didn't I?"

"Yes, earlier today. The one out front? It was hard to make out though. Such an old photo." Connie said.

"Oh! Gosh no! Not that one. That one sucks! I have a much better one that's been digitally enhanced. Of course I don't have it on display since it was altered and not authentic, but the guy who did it does excellent work. This is what he truly looked like." She stood and moved Lex to the warm chair where she had been sitting. Lex stayed curled into a ball, pretending to sleep, but I could see his eyes open as he watched her walk across the room. She dug through a stack of papers and photos and held one up.

"Here we go. This is him! Captain Elias Thorne, of the Mystic Mariner."

Connie and I crowded around the photo with

Nora. Lex stood and stretched, glancing casually towards the picture she held.

All three of us gasped.

The hotel's ghost was none other than Captain Thorne himself. It was a perfect match.

"You're telling me my ancestor is actively haunting your hotel? And chasing women around?"

We'd shaken Nora a little. While she'd managed to live with a banshee and appeared to be uncertain, yet accepting, of the Lex situation, the thought of her great, great grandfather's ghost haunting the hotel seemed to be the thing that got her.

"We can't say one hundred percent for sure, but it definitely looks like him. Right?" Connie said looking at me for confirmation.

"It does," I agreed. I could see Lex nodding his head from the corner of my eye and I shot him a look. He was determined to get us busted.

"Can I meet him?" Nora asked quietly. "Do you think he would talk to me?"

"I don't know. It could be sort of traumatic. I mean, he seemed angry. What with being a ghost, and if it's really him, he's been stuck here for well over a hundred years after a violent death. We've sort of been around ghosts like that before and they aren't always like they were in life. Sometimes they are just mean." I tried to explain it as gently as I could.

We'd grown to like Nora quite a bit and didn't want her to be hurt, either emotionally or physically. Considering how invested she was in her family's legacy, if the Captain was hateful to her, it would be a blow to her research. We certainly couldn't trust the ghost to consider her feelings.

"I think I want to try. I'm going to get a room there tonight. And then I'm going to meet my great, great grandfather." She immediately pulled her cell out and placed a call to the hotel. Listening from the other end, we could tell it was bad news. The place was sold out for the weekend. She would have to wait.

Her disappointment was palpable.

Connie and I exchanged a quick conversation confirming that we were both thinking the same thing.

"If you'd like to stay with us tonight, there's plenty of room," Connie said.

"The couch pulls out into a bed," I added.

Nora's face lit up. "You don't know me, yet that's such a kind offer. I mean, if it's truly not an imposition. It is your vacation and all."

We waved her protesting away.

"I'll leave early in the morning, I promise. Oh

goodness, if I could meet him, that would be amazing."

Another quick psychic exchange between Connie and me yet again confirmed we had the same thoughts. We could only hope the Captain was in a better mood than he was the night before.

We'd finished the bottle of wine, said goodbye to Nora and had plans to see her later that evening for dinner and ghost hunting. As we strolled back to the hotel, my phone buzzed. Devlin was on his way and expected to arrive later that night. We both were still unsure how we felt about him inserting himself into our vacation.

We'd worry about it later. For now, it was time for a mid afternoon nap.

CHAPTER 8

"Captain Thorne! Wait!"

"Come back, please!"

We'd been waiting all night for him to show up and when he finally did, he rushed past us like before. This time, we were able to call him by name. When he heard us, he stopped and returned to our door.

We cowered under his black, empty gaze. I can only imagine how we must have looked to him. Two mid-fifties women wearing sweats and fuzzy socks and a younger woman in jeans and a sweatshirt.

Under his intense stare, Nora lost her nerve and began to shake. She took a few steps backward and grabbed my arm.

"It's okay," I whispered. "I don't think he can hurt us."

As if to prove me wrong, he suddenly grew larger and his image encompassed the entire doorway. He opened his mouth and a low rumble shook our insides.

Nora screamed then covered her mouth.

"Sorry," she said, but the scream had been loud enough to wake the couple across the hall. Of course they couldn't see the Captain's hulking form in front of us.

"Thought we saw a snake," I said. At my lame excuse, they shook their heads and went back to their rooms.

I was about the slam the door shut, when I heard a familiar voice. "There my gals are!" It was Devlin. "And you already have found a new ghost! Perfect!"

He looked the Captain up and down, held his hand out, and introduced himself.

"Devlin McCloud, my good sir. And you are Captain Thorne, I assume?"

The ghost nodded once and Devlin clapped his hands. "Come in, if you can. Can you? Do you need to be invited? No, no that's not right. That's vampires, right gals? Ghosts can come can go as they please."

We moved out of the way and watched with shock as Devlin casually led the ghost into our room as though inviting a neighbor over for drinks.

Nora was about to hyperventilate and I had to use the bathroom. It was a perfect moment to excuse ourselves and regroup.

As we huddled into the bedroom, Connie said, "Well, Devlin's here."

I had so many questions. How did he know who Captain Throne was? When had he arrived? And was he staying on our floor?

"You have to calm down," Connie said to Nora.

I was calm now that I could use the bathroom. Old bladders woken in the middle of the night don't do well. I left the bathroom door open a crack so I could hear what Connie and Nora were saying.

"I am. I think I'm okay. Who is that guy?" She asked.

Connie explained as best she could who Devlin was without going into all the details.

"He's a strange friend, I guess. He's helped us out a few times and while we don't always want him around, he's sort of becoming helpful. And he doesn't seem to have any fear."

She did a good job. That's about the best way to

explain Devlin. He appears out of nowhere, helps out, annoys us, and leaves again.

I finished up and joined them in the bedroom.

"Are they still out there?" I asked.

"I think so," Connie said.

I sent a message to Lex, who was still in the sitting area.

What's going on?

Devlin is making Bloody Marys and the two of them are talking.

The reply, I will admit, caught me off guard.

He's what?

Devlin is making Bloody Marys and they are talking. I don't know how else to say it, Sam. That is what is happening.

Lex was getting testy.

Should we come out?

Yeah, but don't talk. This guy is really old school. Turns out he doesn't like women in pants. That's why he was angry.

I hesitated. Should I tell Connie and Nora that little nugget or keep it to myself? I knew Connie would be indignant. And of course, she wouldn't be wrong. We can wear whatever we want to wear and who does he think he is to judge us? Yet, who he was, was a sea-faring captain from the late eighteen hundreds who probably never saw the women in his life in anything other than skirts and dresses. The changes in fashion through the years probably added to his confusion about where he was and how time was passing. No wonder he was angry. It was yet another thing he didn't recognize and couldn't control.

I decided not to say anything.

"Let's go out. But let's be quiet and find out what Devlin is getting out of him."

They agreed and we cracked the door open slightly. The motion caught Devlin's eye and he nodded and winked at us.

We crept into the sitting room and arranged ourselves on the sofa across from where the captain was holding court.

Lex sat at his right side, on the arm rest. The Captain's hand rested gently on Lex's back. His left hand held a large Bloody Mary with a straw.

I wondered how that would work, but he seemed able to drink it without issue. Nothing came spewing out of his stomach and it didn't go straight through him onto the chair.

"I love cats," he said. "They control the rats on the ships."

"Now who is this?" Captain Thorne asked. He was much calmer now and when his eyes landed on us this time, it wasn't nearly as terrifying.

"These are the two ladies who are staying here

right now," Devlin said. "Connie and Sam." Then Devlin held out his hand to Nora. "I'm afraid I haven't met you officially yet. Devlin McCloud, nice to meet you."

Nora shook his hand. "Hi, I'm Nora Dickson."

"Ladies, huh? Wearing pants like the rest of 'em nowadays. I don't like it," he shook his head slowly. "Just ain't right."

"Well, times have changed, Elias. And things are different. I will need you to remember to speak respectfully to them all, now. Despite how you might feel, they are very important to me and I won't have them disrespected."

Connie reached over with her pointer finger, gently pushed my chin, and closed my mouth for me. I now had even more questions. Who was this? What happened to Devlin? Why wasn't the Captain angry? And what was up with the Bloody Marys?

"I can do that for you, Devlin, my friend. Now, someone here called my name earlier. Why?"

Devlin looked to Connie and me and motioned for us to begin.

With butterflies in my stomach, I asked, "Can you tell us about the night the Mystic Mariner wrecked? What happened?"

The Captain paused and took a slow breath. He took a long sip of his drink and wiped his face with the back of his hand.

"Well, you see, it was stormin' real bad. Waves on Huron were easy fifteen, maybe twenty feet, and the blasted lighthouse wasn't lit. We couldn't tell where we were in relation to the shore. She hit rocks. She went down." The Captain hung his head. "I think a few men survived. At least I hope so. Anyway, I went down with the Mystic. That's all I know."

"Yet, you're here. Do you have any idea how that happened?" Devlin asked.

"I surely don't. Last thing I remember was cursing the name of the lighthouse keeper, that dastardly bugger Silas Hawking, then I swallowed a mouthful of water and next thing I knew, I was here. In this form. Am I a ghost?" He asked.

My heart broke a little as his voice cracked on the last word. No matter how irritable or even how old, it's always hard when a spirit realizes that's what it is. I think on some level, they know, but it's different when they find someone like us who they can talk to. Then when they discover the truth, it's a difficult moment.

"Yes, Captain, you are indeed a ghostly apparition. And it appears you've been wondering these halls for close to a hundred fifty years. Surely you've picked up on some of this? As visitors have come and gone? Different owners?" Devlin wasn't quite as sensitive as I would have been.

"Well, yah, it would seem so. But I don't think

I've been awake the entire time. The banshee wakes me up. The next day I usually don't remember anything. Today was different though," he stroked his beard. "The banshee woke me last night and I guess I stayed put right here."

"You hear the banshee, too?" Nora asked.

The Captain turned his murky black eyes on her and paused.

"Well, I should assume so. Tis' only fair since I brought her here."

"What? You brought her here? How?" Nora scooted to the edge of her seat and leaned towards the Captain.

He looked uncomfortable and took another long pull from the straw in his drink. "This thing is a miracle," he said between sips. "A miracle."

Nora looked at me and then Connie for help. Neither of us were inclined to pressure the Captain to speak, much less tell more about the banshee. I sent a thought to Devlin urging him to ask more questions.

"So, how did you get the banshee? And why?" He asked as he flicked his eyes towards me, one eyebrow raised.

"It was a curse mind you. Since that no-good varmint Hawking couldn't be trusted to keep the lighthouse lit, I decided to do something about it myself. I wanted a way to guard the island and the lighthouse so no one else would ever die like my crew and I did that night. I called her here, and it appears she's sticking around."

"She guards the island? How? People always die when she screeches." Nora said.

"People are going to die anyway. She only announces it. She's the warning that the lighthouse is supposed to be. She doesn't kill anyone. How could she? She's a banshee." Elias laughed. A long, low sound rolled from deep within him. Either he thought Nora's questions were silly or he was very happy with himself for succeeding in bringing the banshee.

"What's funny?" Connie asked, wondering the same thing as me.

"Well, I can't believe it worked," he said. "When I was in port, before that last journey, an old woman approached me. She wore a proper dress," he added with a glance at us. "She gave me a Petoskey stone and warned me to hold onto it dearly. Said there would be a shipwreck and that what I wanted to do was dependent on me having that stone. Of course, I had no idea what she was carrying on about at the time, but I took the stone and stuck it in a pouch around my neck. It must have worked."

Well, that took a turn. I was now completely confused and looked to my friends for clarification. It didn't seem to help. Even Lex had stopped purring and was staring at the Captain, his head tilted slightly.

Devlin, however, was delighted. "A Petoskey stone! Of course. That has to be the key to all of this! Well done, old friend, well done!"

Before we knew what was happening, Devlin stood up along with the Captain and it seemed the night was over. They were saying goodbye while I was still baffled. We hadn't made any progress in solving the Captain's haunting and what we'd learned about the banshee only made me have more questions. Plus, we hadn't told him about Nora yet. And now, there's a stone?

The Captain bid us goodnight and drifted through the door.

"How does he do that but not fall through the chair?" Connie muttered. "I've never understood that."

"Me neither," I agreed.

"Well, we have our answers, don't we!" Devlin was entirely too excited. "We can start in the morning. I'll see you ladies then," he started for the door and stopped at the chorus of objections from Connie and me.

"Wait!"

"Stop! No way!"

Even Lex was standing at attention, trying to get Devlin to stop while keeping his mouth closed tightly.

"What?" Devlin asked.

I didn't even know where to start.

"Okay, first," Connie said. "Devlin, what is a Petoskey stone? And what are we supposed to do now?"

"Right," I added. "You got us a lot of good information, but there is still so much we don't know. We didn't even tell him about Nora. And now there's a stone? And what does that mean for the banshee? And for that matter, the Captain? And what in the world made you decide to make him a Bloody Mary of all things?"

Devlin nodded thoughtfully as we spoke. "Yes, I understand how all of this is confusing if you aren't privy to what I know. Good thing I'm here for you gals. You do need me after all."

As much as I hated to admit it and as much as I hated the way he said it, he was right, at least at this moment. He knew more than we did. It was getting late, but we had to learn what he'd discovered.

He sat back down. "Alright, what do you want to know? Where shall we start?"

Connie sat down as well and leaned forward, her elbows on her knees. "Let's start with what you think we should do tomorrow. You talked like it was obvious, but I'm not sure I follow your thinking."

"We start by going to the lighthouse itself. We need to get our hands on anything we can that tells us about that night, specifically what was going on with the lighthouse keeper. What's his name again?"

"Silas Hawking," Nora added.

"Right! Here's how I see it," Devlin began. "The banshee is here because of what the Captain did as the ship went down. He wanted to ensure that the island was protected, as well as keep other ships safe. He lost trust in the lighthouse keeper so felt he had to do something himself. At the same time, some strange woman met him out of the blue," Devlin raised his hands in a circle for emphasis, "and gave him a Petoskey stone. Now, why would she do that? Why would that randomly happen?"

We all shook our heads. I still didn't understand what a Petoskey stone was and I was pretty sure neither did Connie.

"Because she knew something. She had a premonition that something was going to happen and that he would need protection as well as a little help. She must have been a witch or a seer. Either way, there's a spell at work here. We need to break the spell. Then all the other things will fall into place."

"And we do that by...?" I asked.

"We do that by finding that stone!" Devlin exclaimed.

"And where do we even begin to look?" Connie asked. "Devin this is madness. What are you even saying to us?"

Nora laid her hand on Connie's arm and smiled.

"I know where to look. He's right. That's the answer and it will all be okay."

"And the Bloody Mary?" I asked.

"The Captain didn't want any of the fruity stuff you gals have lying around here so I used tomato juice and added some pepper and a strong pour of vodka. Nothing fruity about that!"

With most of our questions answered, and a plan to meet the next day, I walked Devlin to the door. When we were out of earshot, he whispered, "That mind thing can be our little secret. I won't tell anyone. Promise."

He closed the door behind himself before I could tell him everyone else already knew.

CHAPTER 9

"This is not okay!" I yelled as the boat listed heavily to one side. I felt like I was either going to vomit or pass out or both.

"Hang on," Connie said. "Can you focus on the horizon? That's supposed to help."

I wanted to throat punch her. Focusing on the horizon was the biggest bunch of crap I'd ever heard, and I've heard a lot. All that did for me was highlight how high the waves were and how much the boat was rocking. Everyone else seemed perfectly fine, including the five year old who was watching me closely, waiting for the vomit, no doubt.

We were on a ferry heading to a small island a few miles away. No one lived there since it flooded regularly, but Nora said that made it a terrific place to look for Petoskey stones.

"They are a lot more common in Lake Michigan," she said. "But I've had luck finding them here before. And it makes them even more unique when you find them here."

A quick Google search that morning didn't tell me if Petoskey stones were magical or not, but I did learn they are very interesting. Basically, they aren't true stones but rather fossilized colonial corals from three hundred and fifty million years ago. As tectonic plates shifted, roughly two million years ago, glaciers began to move across the Earth. As a result, the coral polyps were scraped off. So now, what you see on the Petoskey stone is a skeleton of once-living coral polyps. They are six-sided and tightly packed. In the center of each section would be the mouth, and the thin lines that radiate out from the center were the tentacles.

Today's adventure was to visit this small area and look for a Petoskey stone. I mentioned that there were several for sale, either online or in an actual store on the island, but no one was interested in my shopping ideas. They were determined to find one themselves.

Don't get me wrong, I knew that would be extremely cool and I was excited, but it seemed that the timing was a bit off for this rock hunting expedition.

When we finally reached the shore, I stumbled off the boat and resisted the urge to drop to my knees and kiss the ground. The little kid was still watching me with a side eye and I was sure that action would bring out more attention than I wanted.

The guide told us how to look for the stones and what we were looking for and we spread out across the beach, heads bent down, eyes focused on the stretch of sand and rock below us.

I wandered away from the group as I looked. Partly because I wanted a few minutes to myself. I still felt nauseous from the boat and sometimes, the psychic abilities I'd recently discovered in myself were overwhelming. Hearing other people's thoughts was a unique and helpful gift, but it was a constant effort to keep their thoughts out of my head. It was a dance between them blocking me if they suspected I was reading their thoughts, but mostly, people thought loudly and if I wasn't the one doing the blocking, it was constant noise.

Being alone was comforting and rejuvenating.

I felt as though I were being followed though, and turned to look behind me. Sure enough, Lex was playing in the surf, about thirty feet behind me. He saw me turn and waved his paw. I smiled.

Lex understood. He kept his own thoughts to himself and allowed me space, but I still appreciated that he wanted to be close. I was wandering into an area where no one else was.

As I let my thoughts run free and breathed the clean fresh lake air, I once again got a feeling of being watched. I turned back to Lex, intending to invite him to walk with me and talk a little, but when I looked, he was gone.

A small shiver of panic ran through me, but I shook it off. Lex was probably chasing an innocent rodent up a tree or something and would be back soon. I was fine. This area was difficult to reach and there were no other boats here today. But still, the feeling was overwhelming, so I decided to head back towards the group.

After two steps, a stone came tumbling towards me. I noticed it rolling along from the corner of my eye. It was about the size of a tennis ball and landed two feet in front of me.

"Where did this come from?" I muttered as I picked it up. "Oh my gosh!" I looked around desperately for someone else. Did anyone see this?

How did the stone just roll towards me? It was like someone tossed it. The beach was flat.

"Lex?' I called out carefully. "Are you there?"

After no answer, I used my other communication method.

Lex? Can you hear me?

Sam! Come quick. Over here.

Where is 'over here'? Lex what is wrong?

I heard branches break and what sounded like a tussle in the shrubs. I stuck the large stone into a pocket and followed the sounds.

Lex was following an old woman through the underbrush. He was basically stalking her, staying about five feet behind her. She moved painfully slow so there was no chance she was getting away from him and I easily caught up to them both.

"Excuse me?" I said when I saw what was happening.

She sighed then stopped.

"Did you toss this stone to me?" I asked.

"Tell your daemon to leave me alone," she said in an old withering voice.

She already knew about Lex? Did he talk to her?

No! I didn't. Before you go getting angry at me. I didn't say a word. She just knows.

Well at least we were okay on that. But who was this woman?

"He won't hurt you. He doesn't do that. We have some questions. Why did you give me this? Do you want it back?"

She turned her pale blue eyes on me and I took an involuntary step backwards. Her face was lined with a lifetime of stories. Her long grey hair blew in all directions with the wind. She wore a simple dress and was barefoot, her feet were dirty. I realized her eyes were so pale because of cataracts, no doubt caused by decades of sunrises and sunsets. She lifted a gnarled hand and waved me off.

"It's yours," she said.

"But, why?" I asked her. "I mean, thank you. It's beautiful, but why give it to me? I can find one myself, you don't have to give this up."

I held the stone out trying to give it back to her and she shook her head.

She turned and began making her way deeper into the brush.

Lex asked if he should follow her.

"No," I whispered. "I don't think she would like that. I guess she gave me a lovely gift for some reason. Maybe this will be enough to satisfy everyone else and we can head back now."

Lex grunted.

"What? You don't think so?"

"That's not the point of this trip, Sam. I think you have what we all came here for, we didn't realize it at the time."

As we approached the rest of the group, I caught Nora and Connie's eyes and gestured for them to join me. We huddled in a circle and I pulled the stone out of my pocket.

Nora quickly covered the stone in my hand

with her own hands and whispered furtively, "Hide it, now!"

I shoved it back into my pocket and looked around to see if anyone was watching us.

"Why? What's wrong?"

"Where did you get this?" Nora asked. "You didn't just find it. No way. It's polished and it's large."

"Well, this is where it gets a bit strange, but some old woman appeared out of nowhere and sort of tossed it to me."

"Tossed it? Like 'here, catch?' Come on Sam," Connie said.

"This is amazing," Nora added. "This is the stone we came here for. I hoped this would happen. When I went home last night, I looked up some more information about the stones. Captain Thorne was right. There's an old legend about a woman who appears just before you need an extraordinary act to occur. She gives you the stone but nothing else. There are stories all up and down the coastline of not only sailors, but also regular random people finding fully polished stones that seem to simply appear in front of them. And the stories always go on to tell of something that the person then had to do that was exceptionally brave. Sam, you have been chosen. By her giving you this stone, you will have a profound role in all of this."

Fabulous. Exactly what I needed. I didn't even think I'd make it back without making that kid's day and puking all over myself. Now I've got a profound role?

~

We returned to the hotel without incident a few hours later. Breakfast was still in my stomach and a little boy was rather disappointed. Now all I wanted was to lie down for a while and let my stomach settle. Connie offered to make some peppermint tea while I stretched out on the couch.

She and Nora chatted while the water heated.

"What do you think her role is?" Connie asked.

"Hard to say. But we know it's all linked somehow."

"We still need to get into the lighthouse, too. We need to look for anything else that will tell us more about the lighthouse keeper back then. And I'd love to talk to Elias again. Now that we have the stone, maybe he will tell us more."

"Could be talking to him is the brave thing I have to do," I mumbled.

Connie laughed a little too hard, then a sharp tap on the door made my stomach lurch.

Nora opened it to a fully dressed Devlin. He wore his old hat that I hadn't seen in a long time, and a full suit.

"Well, don't you look dapper," Nora laughed.

I wanted to tell her not to encourage him.

"Oh, you are too kind. Lovely, young lady, you have made my day." Devlin gushed.

Connie looked at me and we both rolled our eyes.

"Come on in Devlin, we've got some news."

As we filled him in on the day and the discovery of the Petoskey stone that we now had in our possession, as well as how it came to be in our possession, I sipped my tea and began to feel better almost immediately.

Devlin clapped his hands and nodded along as we took turns telling him of our adventures that morning.

"I had a wonderful day as well," he said. "You know how we need more information about the original lighthouse keeper?"

We nodded.

"And I know you all know that the current keeper, Mayor Alistair doesn't want to tell anyone anything."

Again, we nodded.

"And you know how he knows all three of you, but he doesn't know me?"

"Devlin! Stop playing around. What did you do?" Connie snapped.

"Well," he said, dragging out the word. "I visited him. I said I was from a very well-funded political action committee and that we liked what we saw from him. News of his mayor-ing had reached us and we wanted to talk to him about running for governor."

"And he believed that?" I asked. "Even after you used the word 'mayor-ing'?"

Devlin nodded. A huge smiled stayed on his face.

"Of course he did," Nora said. "You guys have no idea the size of the ego we're dealing with here. Go on," she added.

"When I told him we wanted to support him in a run for governor, he was very excited and almost fell over himself thanking me. I worked a little of my own magic and as we talked, I turned the conversation to scandals and other unsightly situations. I told him we needed confirmation that his background was clean and if there was anything salacious in his history, or in his family's history, he would be best suited to tell me now so we could take care of it."

Devlin paused for a moment, allowing the suspense to grow.

"And?" Nora prompted.

"And he gave me this," Devlin pulled a small old notebook from a bag and laid it on the table. "And this," he followed it with another notebook that had old yellow papers sticking out of it.

"He said there was a bit of a scandal from way

back in the day. He said it had nothing to do with him, but he's lived in fear all this time that someone would discover it and it would destroy any chances he had of making it all the way to the top. After he confirmed that we, and by we, he meant this wealthy group that was on his side, could 'take care of it,' he gave them to me and the fool trusted me with all of this. Whatever his scandal is, it's apparently right here for us to read."

"I knew he had these!" Nora exclaimed.

CHAPTER 10

Nora immediately began reading the journals. As she turned the old, weathered pages carefully, she couldn't help exclaiming.

"This is amazing!"

We'd ask her what she was discovering, but she never answered. I'm not sure she even heard us. She was consumed with the rest of a story that had eluded her for decades.

We busied ourselves quietly until she finally, she sat back and sighed.

"Now I understand," she said.

Connie and I moved closer to where she sat and waited expectantly for the shocking story that would explain the banshee, the curse, and why Captain Thorne was still wandering these halls.

When Nora spoke, it was anticlimactic at best.

"So he was drunk," she said.

"Right, we sort of knew that, right?"

"Yes, but why he was drunk is a whole other story. His family had just died. His wife and newborn within a few days of each other. His wife had a bacterial infection from giving birth, and the baby died from malnutrition most likely. Apparently, Silas didn't know how to care for the baby or his other two children. After she died, he lost his mind with grief. The town took care of the other children until his brother arrived and took them in. He allowed others to help with them, but rejected all help for himself. He was drinking that night, but another tragedy occurred after the shipwreck. Apparently, Silas was so distraught, he killed himself."

"That is very interesting, and sad," I said. "But why would Eli try so hard to keep this from coming out? Why hide the journals?"

"I don't know, but I want to. Let's go ask him," Nora said as she stood, ready to confront her ex.

"Now, wait a second. That's not a good idea," the steady voice of reason came from a most unexpected source.

"Why not, Devlin?"

"Well, if you show up with the journals, he's going to know I wasn't telling the truth and the one thing we have that's making him talk would be gone. We don't want that do we? And we don't want him to find out we are working together."

"Then I'll just ask questions," Nora said.

"What kind of questions?" Connie asked. "It would be strange that hours after giving this man the journals that talk about this, suddenly you show up asking about the very thing that the journals mention."

"She's right," I added. "Let us go. And we'll simply look around and see what we can find out. Maybe he'll talk to us. I doubt it, but it makes more sense that we would be sight-seeing again."

Nora reluctantly agreed. She said she wanted to do more research based on the information in the journals. As she wrapped the books carefully in a towel and stuck them in her bag, she said, "These will go where they've belonged all along. I want to make digital copies so we don't lose the history and then I'll preserve them. This is invaluable to the overall history of the lighthouse and the shipwreck."

We promised to meet up again that evening and share what we'd learned. Nora was getting more excited and hugged us tight before leaving.

When the door closed behind her, Lex asked, "So who's going to be the one to tell Captain Thorne that he died because Silas was drunk and forgot to light the lighthouse?"

None of us answered because none of us

wanted that particular job. And we still hadn't told him about Nora being his great, great grand daughter.

Devlin went back to his room to stay out of Eli's sight and avoid any chance of being seen with us. Lex also decided to stay behind, but he wanted to take a nap. Apparently, frolicking in the lake waves had worn him out.

He was still there for us though. "Be careful. I'll keep my senses open just in case. You might have to yell for me, but I'll wake up. And if you need me, I'll come right away."

We agreed that we would and after another layer of sunscreen, we headed out the door.

The lighthouse was deserted when we arrived. No one else was even in the area.

"This is strange," Connie muttered.

"Is it open?" I asked trying the door.

It opened easily, and we both shrugged as we went in.

"It's not like anyone's going to take anything, right. It's all under glass or it's sort of attached to the wall somehow. I guess leaving it unlocked is normal."

"Didn't Nora say that Eli has an office here? That he converted one of the small rooms?"

"Yeah, I wonder where it is. And maybe that's where he is right now. We just can't see him."

We debated back and forth for a little while, as we looked around the museum part of the lighthouse.

The air inside was different. It smelled like salt and aged wood from over a century ago. The first floor consisted of most of the base which was encircled by steps leading to the annex. Our footsteps echoed slightly in the large room.

We paused in front of various glass enclosed relics that either told a story through words, or items like rusty tools, or photographs of previous keepers, frowning in the seriousness of their jobs.

Nothing had changed from the last time we were here, but it all felt more ominous knowing what we now knew about Eli Alistair, the "current" lighthouse keeper. It wasn't long before we both had seen everything for a second time.

"Want to go back up?" Connie asked. "We could look around again and check if we missed anything last time."

I wasn't sure what she thought we might have missed, but I figured we might as well.

We looked at the narrow staircase, and then looked at each other. With a determined breath, we grasped the smooth handrail, no doubt polished from the generations before that used it to guide their steps. And we began our climb up again. This time it was darker outside so while our first trip up had been well-lit, this one was a bit more treacherous. As we crept along, I was increasingly aware of the wooden stairs creaking underfoot. Connie was in front and would occasionally say something like, "Watch your step." Or, "This one's got a loose spot."

If one of us fell, the entire trip would be worthless not to mention it would likely result in a broken hip or something worse.

"How's your knee?" Connie asked between breaths.

"Okay," I huffed. "Your hip?"

"Starting to flare up, but I'll be okay. I took an anti inflammatory before we left."

"Smart."

As the stairway became tighter and, I don't know how it was possible, but steeper too, I had a moment of claustrophobia and had to pause. Thankfully, we were in front of one of the narrow windows that allowed a sliver of light and air through the dankness.

Through the small window, I could see shadows from the waves in the lake and a tiny bit of the beach glimmered in the setting sun's light.

I breathed deeply trying to calm my racing heart, while Connie leaned against the wall and rubbed her side.

My breath caught, and I had to look again.

"Connie, he's coming," I whispered. I moved away from the window so she could see Eli Alistair walking briskly towards the lighthouse.

"He's almost here. Can we hurry back down in time?" Connie turned and began to scurry down the steep stairs. She'd barely taken three steps before she stumbled and slipped down a few more and around the corner. I couldn't see her.

"Connie!" I was trying to whisper, but the panic in my voice got the better of me and I could hear my own words echoing back to me.

I heard Eli's voice.

"Who's up there?" He said. "This is off limits. You are trespassing. Come down here or I'll call the police."

"Um, it's okay. No need." I said. "We weren't paying attention and got all caught up in the history and all." I was rambling, trying to buy time as Connie gathered herself and stood.

"You're okay?" I asked.

She nodded and straightened her top as she tested first one ankle then the other, then one shoulder and the other.

"Yeah, you know us," Connie added. "We met the other day."

"Hold on, we're coming down," I tried to sound like a chipper tourist who got caught with their hand in the candy jar. Knowing what we knew about Eli's ambitions made him a bit scarier than before, but he didn't know we knew. Hopefully we could laugh this off.

"Gosh, so sorry," Connie said as we rounded the last curve in the staircase.

Eli Alistair wasn't laughing though. He stood with his arms crossed and his legs spread wide, blocking our path.

"Yes, of course. I should have known. Back for some more history now, huh?" He asked.

"Yes, really, we're sorry," I said. "It was my fault. I just love old architecture and I wanted to see more of the lighthouse again. The door was unlocked, so we thought it would be okay. We're sorry. We'll leave now."

I tried to move past Eli, but he didn't budge. A small tingle of panic began in the pit of my stomach. It became a struggle to stay calm. Eli smiled.

You would think that would have made me feel better, but there was something sinister behind his smile. It wasn't genuine. It was menacing.

"No. Don't leave. If you're so interested in all of this, let's take a tour. I've nothing to hide here, yet you seem to think I do."

"What? No, of course not. Why would we think that?" I asked.

"I've seen you with Nora. And I have people on the island who are loyal to me. I've heard about the questions you've been asking and the places you've been to. Did you find a Petoskey stone on your outing earlier today?" He said the last part in a teasing sing-song voice that made no sense to me.

"Unfortunately, no," I lied as I gripped the stone in my pocket. It was a decent size, but way too fragile to be any sort of weapon. Of course, based on what the Captain and the old woman said, I didn't think it was supposed to be a physical weapon.

"Well, come on then," Eli said as he stepped slightly to the side. Using his arms he corralled us into the annex that we'd unknowingly passed earlier. In seconds, we found ourselves in Eli's private office.

Connie and I have been around for a while and we both knew without a doubt that going into that room with Eli was a mistake. Be assured, one that neither of us would ever have made that decision were we alone. But together, we didn't always make the best choices, and buoyed by a false sense of security, we found ourselves in a small, tight room with our backs to the wall opposite the door. Eli stood in front of the door and blocked any chance of escape.

As the bile began to build up even more in my gut, Eli surprised us both when he flipped on the radio and sat down behind his desk.

"Have a seat," he gestured to two straight back chairs. "Sorry I don't have anything more comfortable. Oh, hey, listen," he turned the radio up and put his finger to his lips.

The weather report was on and told of a potential storm crossing the state. When the announcement was finished, I asked about the storm's path.

"Will it hit here?" I pulled my phone from my pocket intending to access my familiar weather app.

"Possibly, that's why I wanted to come in here. I wanted the NOAA weather radio and access to the GLERL report."

"GLR... the what?" Connie asked.

"The Great Lakes Environmental Research Lab. They monitor storms and their impact on lake conditions. I also have some men who report in from various places on the lake and inland. If this hits just right, it could be pretty bad."

"Oh, well, I guess we should be going. Let you handle this without us being in the way, and I suppose we should get to safety ourselves. Just in case."

"Why don't you stay here for a little while longer," Eli said standing to block the door again. "Just in case."

"I'm not getting reception in here," I said. "Connie, can you?"

"Cell reception here is notoriously bad," Eli

said. "Here, give me your phones and I'll put them over here. Sometimes reception will come through closer to this window."

"No, that's okay. We don't need reception right now. We'll just-"

"Give them to me, I said." He held his hand out and stared at us. "Just in case."

This guy was getting on my nerves. He scared me to death, but he was also so weird and cryptic. Was he angry? Or was he distracted? Did he mean to be so menacing?

"Just in case of what?" Connie asked, also standing. Guess she was feeling much like I was.

"Sometimes these storms come on fast. I don't want you to get caught out there without someone else knowing where you are. Let's try to get service here, then you can inform the hotel when you're on the way back. But first, let me gather some more information. Please, I'd hate for you to be harmed. And let me make it interesting for you. A little more incentive to stick around." He said with a tight smile as he reached down under his desk.

He has a gun!

My silent words shot into Connie's brain at the same time she sent an equally terrified message to me.

He's going to shoot us!

In the split second it took for those thoughts to

ping between us, Eli pulled out a small chest and set it on his desk.

Connie and I covered the fact that we had both jumped, and I think Connie squeaked a little.

By now I had to use the bathroom frantically. But what he showed us made all of that disappear into the background.

It was a rolled up scroll.

"This is my pride and joy," he said. "You'll never guess who I am."

CHAPTER 11

The storm hit as promised. As each gust of wind caught at us, ripping our hair and clothes all around, I tried desperately to reach Lex.

We're trapped at the top of the lighthouse. Help!

Over and over again, I sent him the message. I even tried to tap into Devlin's mind. Then I tried Nora's. None of them worked. I couldn't get through.

Eli tricked us after all. The scroll was indeed a fascinating item. Connie and I poured over it trying to absorb the names and locations as we applied all of the knowledge we already had.

It all made perfect sense when we realized we were looking at a family tree. A family tree that started a few generations before Silas Hawking and ended with our very own Eli Alistair.

"You're related!" I exclaimed. "That's fascinating. Why haven't you told anyone else?" I asked.

It seemed like a strange secret to be so determined to keep. I was pretty sure a lot of people on the island had family that was there for generations and while Silas's crime was particularly awful, it didn't have any baring on Eli. It's not like he was the one who didn't light the flame, right?

Eli didn't view it that way.

"It was my family though. Do you understand the guilt that I carry around with me from this? I destroyed the ship. Or well, he did. Silas."

Freudian slip or overly stressed man misspeaking? I chose to go with Freudian slip and that's exactly why we were in this position.

"Sorry, Connie," I said as another gust of wind blew salty rain into our faces. The temperature was dropping and we were soaking wet. If we didn't get struck by lightning first, the pneumonia we'd both end up with might be what killed us.

"Why? You didn't do this?" She said.

"Well, it was my big mouth," I replied. I used air quotes to mock myself. "Hey! What do you mean 'I destroyed the ship?' What did you do Eli? Why do you have guilt?"

He never answered us because the banshee let out a piercing and mournful wail that went on for several seconds. Eli went into action.

"Come on," he said. And he pulled out the gun

that we accurately suspected he was hiding all along. "Now that you know my secret and the banshee is wailing, let's give her two lives to take tonight."

He nudged us towards the door and up the steep, narrow stairs to the very top, which is where we now huddled. Our cellphones were locked in his office and a large, heavy wooden door was bolted closed at the top of the stairs.

The banshee wailed again, and I jumped.

"Remember, she doesn't wail because she's going to kill someone. She wails as a warning that someone is going to die."

"I don't understand how that's supposed to comfort me," I said to Connie.

"Because, someone was going to die anyway. It's not us, Sam," she said. "We're uncomfortable and will have colds for sure, but this isn't something to die from. She's wailing for someone else."

I hoped she was right.

As the evening wore on and the lightning and thunder intensified, I wasn't as confident in Connie's words. We were both shivering uncontrollably by now. It didn't help that despite being surrounded by rain and water, both of us were thirsty and hungry. Once the rain started, we took turns peeing, trying to aim for the edge, but any that might have spilled over was washed away in the rain. Then came the job of getting our bottoms pulled back on.

Wet denim pulled over a wet middle-aged bottom was an exercise in extreme patience and humility.

"I'm losing weight when we get back home," Connie said.

I'd agreed at the time, but now I was starting to wonder if we would make it back home. I didn't understand why I couldn't reach Lex or even Devlin. Lex said he'd be listening for me and he had to know about the storm. With us not back yet, why weren't they looking for us? Surely they were worried. Even Nora hadn't heard from us the rest of the day and we had plans to meet tonight.

Where had everyone gone? And what was going on?

Connie and I huddled together with our backs to the storm trying to conserve body heat. The wind whipped around so aggressively it was impossible to determine which direction it came from. With our heads bent together we tried to distract each other.

"I still don't understand why he's so paranoid about people knowing he's related to Silas," she said.

"I feel like he was going to tell us, but this started," I said between what felt like buckets of water splashing my face.

A gust of wind blew so hard, it knocked us sideways and I gripped the railing for fear of being washed over the side. We were sliding now with each strong gust of wind. The smooth wooden floor was covered by at least two inches of water. We'd tried the door to the apex multiple times but it was locked solid.

As another gust of wind blew me to the side, something jabbed my thigh. I reached into my wet pocket and managed to fish out the Petoskey stone the old woman had gifted me earlier that day.

"I'm glad you lied to him when he asked about that," Connie said nodding towards the stone. "He might have taken it or something."

"So? Not like it's doing us any good right now."

"Wait," Connie said. "Are you sure? What was it the Captain said about the stone the old woman gave him? Remember? That it would give him the power to do what he needed to do when the time was right."

Her look was expectant and hopeful. I hated to crush her spirits, but I did anyway.

"If you're waiting for me to do something amazing because the time is right or something, no one has told me about it. Your faith is sorely misplaced."

Her face fell, but then she smiled. "Nah, I don't think so. The Captain had no idea what his strength was going to be and neither do you. I don't think you're supposed to know."

Oh, dear, sweet Connie. Wonderful naive, precious Connie. She had no idea how clueless and hopeless this was. Our best bet would be getting rescued in the morning, and we could only hope we didn't slide off the top of the lighthouse or drown in the deluge before someone found us.

I left her to her thoughts and she left me to mine. My mind wandered through the events on the island and how everything that we planned always seemed to go sideways. I spent a lot of emotional and mental energy trying to make things happen a certain way, but no matter how hard I tried, heck even when I didn't try and I forced myself to relax and allow things to happen naturally, they still went poorly.

It's like there was some plan that as soon as I hit forty, everything would start going downhill. That entire decade sucked. But I wasn't in my forties anymore. Now halfway through my fifties, things were better. So many things had changed recently, I had to remember the positive.

I reminded myself to focus on what was real and true. What I knew to be a fact. The people and the things I knew I could count on. I wasn't the same person I was in my forties, I didn't struggle to see clearly any more. The veil over my eyes had lifted, and I could clearly see...

Wait!

I elbowed Connie in the ribs.

"Look, the storm stopped."

She turned to me, her eyes wide as her hair flew around behind her. She looked like a sea witch, and I laughed.

"Sam," she whispered. "Are you okay?"

"Yeah, of course, look! The storm has stopped. It's okay. Gosh, look at the moon. Connie, what's wrong?"

She wasn't looking at the sky, she was looking at me. The look of horror on her face was worrisome and I wondered which of us was losing it.

But I looked around again and I knew what I saw. The rain was gone. The sky was clear and the moon shone brightly. Even my clothes and my hair were dry.

I still held the Petoskey stone in my hand, and I looked at it. Was that the key?

I held Connie's hand with the hand that held the stone and waited.

Carefully, she began to look around as well. She shook her head and her dry hair moved in the breeze.

"It stopped?" She said.

"I don't think it ever happened."

"But how? Why?"

"I don't know. But I can hear Lex calling. He's wondering when we'll be home. He's hungry for dinner."

Still not sure what to expect, we carefully stood and stretched. Connie tried the door which opened easily. We made our way back down the steep stairs. My thighs were burning and my calves beginning to cramp, but we didn't stop to rest at all.

"How many steps do you think there are?" I asked.

My mildly obsessive friend answered easily, "Two hundred and ten."

Thankfully, the door at the bottom of the stairs swung open much easier than we expected, and we tumbled into the museum area. It was still deserted and there was no sign of Eli.

"We need to check on Nora," I said.

Connie agreed and after a quick stretch to work through another Charlie horse, we set off for Nora's.

CHAPTER 12

"Oh thank goodness!" She said when she opened the door. "I've been trying to reach you. You aren't answering your phones."

"Well, we have a reason for that," I said. "Eli took them away from us and then locked us in the lighthouse. There was a terrible storm, or I guess somehow he made us think there was a storm? It was strange."

Connie picked up where I left off. "It was like only we could see the storm and we thought all these things. Like we were stuck up there and were going to die. And the banshee! Did you hear the banshee?"

Nora nodded. "Yes, twice. So you did too?"

We nodded.

"Well, there was no storm. No rain. Nothing.

How did you figure it out? No! Wait, the Petoskey stone, right? Somehow it helped you see what you needed to do, or I guess what you needed to see in this case. I can't believe Eli did this to you, but it makes sense. The journals I've read explain it all. He comes from a very evil family."

"Yes, we know! He showed us a scroll with his family tree on it. He's related to Silas Hawking."

We explained to Nora what the scroll and what Eli himself had told us about the relationship. He was the great great grandson of Eli. The great grandson of one of the boys that the island adopted.

"Who on the island adopted the boys?" Nora asked. "Did he tell you?"

"He didn't tell us, but I'll bet it's on that scroll and we just didn't look for a name. We weren't sure what we were looking at and then everything went sideways and well, you know, the fake storm that almost killed us and everything." I shrugged.

"Sure, right. I get it. We need that scroll. I want to know who adopted him. How did he create that storm in your minds and make you think that? I wonder if Eli is the reason for the deaths on the island? But why would he want to harm you?"

"Oh, he had plenty of opportunity to harm us. He had a gun, Nora. He could have shot us!"

"But he wanted it to look like an accident," she

squinted as she thought. "You know, there have been a few cases of people jumping from the lighthouse over the decades. It's unusual enough that I remember a few of them. Now I'm starting to wonder if they jumped intentionally, or if it was the same thing that happened to you. I think the family possesses some sort of magic or something. I read in one of these journals that Silas refused to participate in the evil things his family did, but when he died and his brother raised the boys...," her voice trailed off.

"It's terrifying to think that Eli has access to that kind of power," I said.

"And is so determined to use it in order to protect himself. And from what?" Connie added. "What in the world is he trying to protect?"

We agreed that those were all good questions and before we could delve any further, into them, I heard Lex again.

I am dying of starvation. I'm going to the restaurant and look for dinner.

In what was yet another very cat-like behavior, Lex at times availed himself of the dumpster outside of seafood restaurants. No matter how many times we'd offered to bring him food, when he was hungry, he didn't want to wait. He insisted that he arrived immediately after food had been dumped.

"Usually it's still warm," he said once.

Thoroughly disgusted, Connie and I tended to ignore those types of comments.

"I'm hungry," I said. "Shall we grab some dinner, out in public where we can be seen?"

I was worried about Eli being out there. Probably thinking we were still locked up on the lighthouse and possibly even dead. What would his reaction be when he saw us alive and well?

Neither of us was anxious to find out.

Several townspeople had wandered to Nora's when they heard the banshee's wails. Nora stopped them in their tracks this time and before they had a chance to begin demanding answers, she asked a few questions of her own.

"Who here remembers the children of Silas Hawking? Anyone grow up hearing stories about them? Or does anyone know anything?"

"Why are you asking about those no-goods," Clem asked. The old man we'd seen when we first arrived was standing in his usual spot, leaning against the wall.

"Clem, do you remember them?"

"Not well. Mostly I remember my mother telling me to stay far away from them. That family had some sort of magic about them. People always died when they were around. Starting with their own mother and little brother. Then their father," Clem explained. "They say he killed himself over grief from the shipwreck, but it was grief from the mother dying too. But those boys were involved either way. That family has finally died out thank goodness."

"Well, I'm not so sure. It seems our own Mayor Alistair might be related to them."

The sounds of gasps and coughs wafted through the room as everyone took in this new information.

"But before we get all worked up and try to ask him about it, you have to realize he's dangerous. We are working with spiritual and supernatural things. The banshee was actually here to warn us of what Eli and his family were doing. The banshee warns us not when there's going to be a death, rather she warns us when there's going to be a murder." Nora's dramatic statement garnered the reaction she hoped for and the crowd gasped and grew silent.

"She wailed twice tonight. Did two people die?" Someone whispered.

I nudged Connie. "I'll bet those were supposed to be for us."

"Bet you're right," Nora agreed. She raised her voice for the crowd to hear. "The banshee wailed for these two," she told them. "But they survived with the help of a Petoskey stone given to one of them by the old crone on the small island."

I expected her strange words would cause some sort of a riot, yet everyone seemed to accept them as the truth. Most were nodding along and agreeing with her every word as though understanding a long held secret that made perfect sense.

"We're going to set things right soon. Will you trust me? Will you trust the great great granddaughter of Captain Elias Thorne of the Mystic Mariner to do what must be done to save our island?"

"This is it," Clem whispered. "Yes, I trust you."

And with those words, the rest of the crowd began to disperse with promises to spread the word, to be on the lookout for Mayor Alistair and consider him dangerous. And then, to listen for next steps.

Nora stopped Clem and waited while everyone left. When we were alone, she turned to him.

"Clem, we need your help. What do you know about the boys who were adopted? What did they do?"

Nora led us into the back area of the center and settled Clem in an old chair. When he was comfortable, he rubbed his eyes and began to tell a story.

"I never talked about this before because I thought it was all over. But after what you said about Alistair being of that family, I think I have to say what I know. Or what I think I know. It's a long story and one I've heard told in my family ever since I can remember."

"What's the story, Clem?" Nora asked.

"Those boys were evil, for sure. The entire family was evil, except Silas. Poor Silas and his wife were innocent in all of this."

"I don't know that I'd say he's innocent. He is the reason the ship wrecked and all those men lost their lives. All because he was drunk."

"It wasn't his fault, though," Clem said. "It was the boys. They inherited the curse that followed that family. Some say it was magic. Some say it was a deal with the devil himself. I don't know," he said again, shaking his head. "All I know is that when the boys became teenagers, people started dying. Then they started getting richer and richer. Rumors are they even got married and had kids of their own, but no one ever saw them. They always kept to themselves in the woods. My grandmother told me once that she and a friend were wandering out there and she swears she watched at least ten kids running around. But no one in town ever believed her because no one ever saw them."

"Is that why you thought the family had died out? They never came into town, so eventually, you came to believe they were gone?" I asked.

"And no one ever checked on them? I understand the men were dangerous, but there were children. And what about the women they married? Who were they?"

"Now you're asking questions I can't answer young lady," Clem said to Nora. "I'm saying what I've heard and that's all."

"I understand. Please go on. Do you know anything else that might help us?"

Clem continued explaining that Silas was considered the black sheep of his family because he didn't participate in what was happening. He didn't use magic or anything else and he wasn't greedy.

"He had a brother though. That's who took those boys. You wanted to know that. The brother took them and disappeared with them into the woods after Silas died."

I looked at Connie and raised an eyebrow. This story perfectly matched what she and I had learned, as well as what Nora discovered in the journals. It seemed we were getting some answers.

"How do you think Eli came to be? How come he's not out in the woods living like the rest of the family? Didn't he go to college out of state?" Connie asked.

"I would suspect, as times changed, so did they. According to the rumors, they had a lot of money and a lot of power, supernatural and otherwise. And don't let the fact they lived feral make you think they weren't smart. You've seen Eli. Someone had to teach him, right?"

I shivered involuntarily. "Do you think more of them are out there right now? Still living in the woods?"

The old man shook his head. "Naw, I was right when I said the family had died out. Well, except for Eli now, of course. That was a surprise. So, let me back up. I'm saying there aren't any more out in the woods. The government owns that land now. But, are there more like Eli out there somewhere else? That I can't say."

"I can't believe I almost married him. Can you imagine what might have happened?"

"It would have been terrible. It explains a lot though, doesn't it? Why he's so angry with you for ending it. That must have hurt his ego," I said.

"And probably affected his plans. If he is the last of his family, he needs children to carry on," Connie added.

"And it explains why his political moves are so important. He's using his power to gain more and more power. That's why he went after you two. He knows you understand so much more than everyone else. He can manipulate the people on the island, but being from the outside makes you more dangerous to him. You could expose him," Nora was pacing now.

"It's a crazy story, though," Connie said. "Who

would believe us? Like you said, we're strangers from the outside."

Clem piped up. "You'd be surprised. I'd say not every single person on the island has heard about that family, but you'd be hard pressed to find someone here who doesn't believe in the hoodoo that goes on around here. These are folks who've lived their entire lives hearing a banshee wail and then the very next day learning of someone's death. Whether by unusual means or not, it's still going to affect you."

"Clem is right," Nora said. "We can tell them what we we've learned and I promise, they will believe us. And that is what scares Eli Alistair so much."

When we arrived at the condo, we ate a late dinner and waited for Lex and Devlin. We filled them both in on what had happened that afternoon.

Lex was adamant that neither of us leave without him again. Even Devlin appeared shaken when we got to the part about the gun.

"This is serious," he said in the understatement of the day.

We still wanted to talk to the Captain again. While our last visit was informative, we had so many more questions for him and he needed to know the full story behind the lighthouse that night. Not to mention, we needed to tell him who Nora was.

"I have an idea," Devlin said. He mixed a Bloody Mary and placed it in the hallway, just outside the door. "That's the strangest ghost trap I've ever laid."

It may have been the strangest, but it was also very effective. In less than five minutes, the Captain drifted through our door.

It was still disconcerting to be minding your own business and turn around to see him, floating in the air, his coat tails waving up and down and those black eyes watching you.

Once we recovered from his sudden arrival, he settled into his chair and Nora retrieved his drink from the hallway. We had a pretty long list of things to talk to him about, but the very first thing was Nora. We decided Devlin would do the introductions since the Captain seemed to like him best.

"Captain," Devlin began, "we have something to tell you. I think you will be pleased."

Between long sips of his drink, he said, "Yah, what is it?"

Devlin motioned for Nora, and as she stood beside him, he said, "You've already met Nora, but what you don't know is she's your great, great granddaughter."

The Captain lowered the glass to the table. His eyes bore into Nora's. She held her ground, smiling a little uneasily but not backing away. Something was happening to the Captain's eyes. It appeared he was beginning to cry as the black orbs shimmered. They began to change from coal black to crystal blue. The same color as Nora's eyes.

"You do look like her. Yah, I see it," his voice trembled.

Nora smiled. "I think I resemble my great, great grandmother. But it looks like I have your eyes."

Despite all the things that happened that day, this was a beautiful moment and one that deserved all the time it needed. We gave them privacy as Nora shared as much about Elias Thorne's family as she could. She told of how his brave wife and children carried on after his death and what that meant to the generations of family that followed.

As they spoke, Devlin, Lex, Connie and I quietly made our way onto the balcony. The evening was mild, almost a chill in the air, but after what Connie and I had just experienced, it was beautiful.

Lex curled into my lap and pressed himself to me.

"You aren't cold are you?"

"Nah, no. Not a bit. I thought you might be and wanted to keep you warm."

I smiled at his lie and ignored it. I liked it when he snuggled, no matter the reason.

"It would be helpful to get our hands on Eli Alistair's family tree again. That scroll holds more answers for us and it's proof of the relations." Connie started the conversation.

"True. But it would be good to talk to the banshee," Lex said.

We all stopped talking and looked at Lex.

"Are you nuts?" I asked. "How? And what would we say?"

"We'd hear her side of this," Lex explained. "She was summoned by the Captain and has been doing her job all these years. She might want to be released. Have you thought of that?"

"But then who would warn the island? Remember? She warned the island when Eli's ancestors were doing harm, and for that matter, we're pretty sure she's warning them when Eli himself is up to no good."

"Let's think about this for a second though," Lex said thoughtfully. "We know she only wails as a warning. But what if she didn't have anything to warn the island about? She arrived after a tragedy, and stayed because of Alistair's evil family. What if the evil family wasn't here any longer? Would she leave?"

"What are you saying, Lex, buddy?" Devlin lowered his voice. "Do you think we should you know, 'take care of' Alistair?" Devlin made air quotes.

When his words sank in, Connie and I exclaimed at the same time.

"No!"

"Absolutely not!"

"We aren't killing anyone. Devlin, what is wrong with you?" I hissed.

"Just floating an idea out there, don't get your knickers in a bunch," he huffed.

Lex added, "No, no, not at all. Not kill him, of course, but make him leave. Can we prove what he's done? Tie him to any of the deaths or force him to confess." Lex looked from one to the other and eventually said what he meant. "Have him arrested. Jailed."

"He has the authorities in his pocket," Connie said.

"Yeah, but not the people who live here. Remember what Clem said? There are a few that are loyal, but Nora is convinced most of the people here don't like him very much. I think we need to rely on the people here."

CHAPTER 13

Nora and Captain Thorne were laughing when we entered the room. It was heart-warming to see them getting along that way and it made us all smile. The atmosphere felt lighter and less hopeless than it had a few minutes earlier.

While we hated to bring up more serious topics, we had to act quickly before Eli either hurt someone else or disappeared.

"We found out a lot more about Silas Hawking's family," Nora began. She told the Captain about the family's evil history right down to include Eli Alistair and her own brush with him. She also told him of the lighthouse keeper's grief at losing his wife and child.

"It doesn't change anything," Nora assured her great, great grandfather. "It was still wrong, and it cost so many innocent lives. But surely you under-stand that he was overcome with grief?"

Captain Thorne nodded solemnly. "Yes, I can see that. Like you said, it doesn't make it okay that I lost my crew that night. All those good men. But it does change how I view him, I suppose. He wasn't a no-good loser. He had his own demons."

"Exactly," I said. "So now, we have another question."

The Captain turned his still crystal blue eyes on me and waited. I lost the words I was going to say and stumbled over myself a bit under his intense gaze.

"We are trying to understand why the banshee is here," Nora said, coming to my rescue.

"I suppose she's here because I called her," he said bluntly.

"Right, but she doesn't stop anything from happening. It's more like she announces the deaths, but by then, it's too late," I said.

The captain nodded as I spoke. "Yes, that sure is a puzzle. I don't have an answer for you." He said with a shrug.

"Show him, Sam," Devlin said in a theatrical whisper.

I rolled my eyes and pulled the Petoskey stone from my pocket. I held it out for the Captain.

His eyes grew large and he began to laugh.

"Well, there you go," he said. "That right there is your answer!"

~

I didn't get it. I looked at Connie and could tell by the look on her face that she didn't get it either.

Devlin started laughing along with the Captain. That most definitely did not help.

I shot him a look and he stopped laughing.

"Explain, please." I said.

"The banshee isn't here because she's a warning. She's here because of the stone! The stone is the protection and the banshee is the warning that protection is needed. It's up to the people here to heed the warning and call on the protection." Nora explained excitedly.

Connie jumped in. "So when she gave Sam the stone, it was to protect us from Eli. We had to heed the banshee's warning and use the stone in order to save ourselves."

"So the banshee is like a wake-up call to the island that danger is imminent and they need to save themselves. Just like a lighthouse would warn sailors that they are approaching danger and need to change course?"

"Yes," Nora said. "And because sometimes, the danger is too extreme, the stone intensifies the power already within and empowers the holder to perform extraordinary feats.”

“Has there ever been a time when she’s wailed but no one died?” I asked.

Connie looked at me. “Um, yeah,” and she wiggled her finger between the two of us.

“Well, sure, obviously us. Duh.” I was exasperated. “I’m wondering about anyone else? Wondering if we are the only ones to ever be given the stone and if so, why us?”

“Yes, of course! Many times she’s wailed and nothing bad happened. It could be that whoever she was wailing for was able to overcome whatever the tragedy was.” Nora paused then chuckled. “You know, the banshee wailed the night I broke up with Eli.”

I got chills when she said that. It was just as we theorized. The banshee warned Nora of Eli’s evil, and whether or not she knew it at the time, Nora saved herself by breaking up with him.

“You didn’t have a stone, though,” Connie said.

Nora smiled. “I didn’t need it.”

“Okay, but why did Eli attack us?” I asked. “Why are we threatening to him when it’s the people here who he should fear?”

“Well, none of this would be happening if it weren’t for you two. Maybe it’s the perfect storm,” she glanced at the Captain. “Sorry! Maybe it’s super good timing. You are someone who could interact with the Captain, and talk to him. Without that, we never could have tied everything together," Nora said.

"And we are able to handle all of this," Devlin added. "We are special you know. Not everyone is as comfortable with the other worldly things we get into."

I huffed at Devlin's use of the word "we" in all of this, but what he said wasn't entirely wrong.

Nora echoed my thoughts. "Everything aligned."

We all lapsed into silence as we thought about the extraordinary coincidence.

"She must be so sad," the Captain said out of the blue. "All she can do is wail but she can't change anything or make any difference."

"But she can now," Nora said standing. "We are all here now and things are falling into place but we have to act quickly." She was animated and determined. "This is our chance to set the banshee free. To set you free," she nodded towards her grand father. "And to set the people here free from fear. If our family is destined to stop Eli Alistair and his evil line, then I'm the only left who can do it."

With those brave words, Nora packed up her belongings and prepared to leave.

"I have calls to make and plans to arrange. I'll be in touch tomorrow." She made towards the door and stopped. When she turned back, she smiled softly at the Captain and said, "I'm so glad I got to meet you."

As the door closed behind her, the Captain nodded towards Devlin, Connie and me.

"I expect you'll be keeping that child safe."

And without another word he disappeared.

"No pressure," Lex mumbled.

CHAPTER 14

We passed another hour, sitting on the balcony unwinding from the day. The beach was deserted and it seemed everyone in the hotel was already asleep. It was quiet and almost completely dark with just a sliver of moon for light. The wind had finally died down and it was still.

"I feel like Eli is sitting in the lighthouse watching us," Connie said. "Like he's plotting and stalking or something."

Devlin attempted to put an arm around Connie's shoulders and she shrugged him off. Undaunted, he said, "I will protect you gals."

We both sighed. What were we going to do with this guy?

Lex popped into my mind.

I will protect you.

I know, Lex. We both do. Thank you.

I smiled at him and he winked. We passed the rest of the evening watching the waves gently lap at the shore while we sipped on Connie's mescal margaritas. Even Lex lapped some out of a bowl. It wasn't long before we took turns yawning.

We convinced Devlin that we were safe in our room and sent him off to his own room for the rest of the night with a promise to call him as soon as we woke up.

This was the second late night we'd had and the lack of a solid night's rest was was bound to catch up with us eventually. Even though the events of that day hadn't actually happened, our bodies and minds thought it did and I feared tomorrow would be an achy day no matter how long we were able to sleep in.

Thankfully, it wasn't quite as bad as I feared. I awoke the next morning to the smell of bacon and coffee. Not a bad way to start the day at all.

Connie was standing at the stove flipping bacon and sipping coffee.

"How long have you been up?" I asked. "Did you sleep okay?"

"Yeah," she said. "I slept soundly! And I only got up about twenty minutes ago. I slept for seven hours."

I looked at the clock. She was right. I had a

solid seven and a half under my belt and felt pretty good.

"Must have been all that fresh lake air last night," I said pouring my coffee.

"Don't forget to text Nora," Connie reminded me. "And, Devlin too, I guess."

"Yeah, I'll do it now."

As I texted both of them that we were awake and getting ready for the day. Lex wandered in from the balcony where he'd been bird watching.

"How's it out there?" Connie asked him.

"Beautiful. Not hot, not cold. Nice breeze. Sunny. Pretty much perfect."

As I hit send for Devlin's message, my phone rang. I jumped and dropped it on the table with a loud clang.

"Phones ring, Sam," Lex said wryly.

"Well, I didn't expect it to right then while I'm holding it!" I retorted.

I took a deep breath and tried to return my heart rate to normal. I pressed the green button.

"Hey, Nora, you're on speaker. Good morning."

"Hey everyone," she said. "I've got some news. I talked to Clem and gave it some thought and I think we have a plan. Tonight I'm organizing an event on the beach. It'll be a rally for Eli to support his run for governor. I'm also going to let him believe I want to get back together. The hope is, the banshee will wail and warn us all and then everyone can see what kind of person Eli really is."

"Nora, that is so risky," I said.

"And what exactly do you expect Eli to do? How will the banshee wailing make anyone believe Eli is a snake. What if he behaves himself?"

"Those are good questions, and honestly, I don't have an answer. I just know we have to get Eli and the town together and someone needs to be in danger. We need witnesses."

"I don't like it. You are making yourself very vulnerable. Are you sure?" Connie added. She set the bacon down and removed the pan from the stove as she stared at the phone.

"Yeah, I'm sure," Nora said. "It will work. It has to. Come over when you can. I'll fill you in on the rest. And bring Lex, okay? We need him."

She disconnected the call and as the line went dead, Connie and I looked at Lex.

"What did you do?"

"Nothing," he said.

"Why would she say that?"

"How should I know?"He asked.

"Lex...?"

"Okay, okay. She knows I talk."

"Lex!" We both exclaimed at the same time. Honestly, he had absolutely zero control. It seemed we were traveling around all the time announcing that we had a talking daemon cat with us no matter how discreet we tried to be.

"She figured it out on her own," he protested. "I didn't tell her until she asked. I promise. And she wasn't freaked out. She could tell and she told me it was okay. What was I supposed to do? Lie?"

"Yes!" We both said.

Nora was ready for us when we arrived a few hours later. She had just said goodbye to Clem and was gathering some other items we would need for the rally that night.

She hugged each of us in turn and wiggled her finger between Lex and us.

"They know," he said.

"Oh, good. Are you mad?" She asked.

"No, but are you sure you're okay? Most people don't react well to Lex. You seem to be taking a talking cat in stride."

"You guys have got to realize it's like what Clem said yesterday. When you grow up hearing a banshee wail, you get used to unusual things happening. And after meeting the ghost of my ancestor, this is nothing. Plus, Lex is the best. And he is so smart." She reached down and scratched him behind the ear.

Lex puffed himself up and grinned at us. This

was just what we needed. Feed his ego even more. Her words went straight to his head.

"Where's Devlin?" Nora asked.

"He's staying hidden until we are ready for him. Since Eli thinks Devlin is on his side and wants to help him with his political ambitions, he shouldn't be seen with us at all. In fact, we shouldn't be seen either," I said.

"Right. Better he think you're dead or were so scared that you left. Actually, that's what we're counting on," she said. "Okay, let me fill you in on the plans."

Nora went on to explain that she and Clem were calling on the residents of the island to join them tonight to support their local candidate for governor, Mayor Eli Alistair.

"We aren't telling all of them what we're doing though. We're counting on the fact that Eli will show his true self and everyone will see for themselves."

"And we're counting on the banshee to wail, right? What if she doesn't?"

"I'm convinced she will. I'll be in danger, and ...," she paused, looking at Connie and me expectantly.

I didn't like where this was going.

"Once Eli sees you and realizes you both are still alive and are right there on the beach, he's going to be furious. He only told you his secrets because he thought he could, well, you know, get rid of you somehow. When he realizes you are still here and are most likely telling everyone what he did, if he isn't already angry, he will be then."

"So we are bait," I said.

"In a sense," Nora said, "We all are going to be the bait."

"And how will Devlin convince him to show up?" Connie asked.

"He'll tell him that this is a rally for him. That the people on the island want to support his run for governor and that this is all for him," Lex said. "According to Nora, his ego is big enough, he'll believe it. And she won't say so, but come on, we know he'll do anything Nora asks of him, especially if he thinks that will win her back. So if he finds out that she set this rally up for him, he'll be here."

"Then he'll find out that Connie and I are alive and everything will go sideways and we become walking targets," I said.

"Honestly, he already has to know you're still alive, right? They didn't find your bodies at the base of the lighthouse, or anywhere else for that matter." Lex helpfully added.

"My guess is he believes he scared you away," Nora said tapping her chin.

Hoping that was indeed what he was thinking, if he was thinking about us at all, we decided to keep a low profile for the rest of the day. Nora found us two outrageous floppy hats that we pulled low over our faces and we returned to the hotel as quickly as possible.

When we arrived safe and sound, we collapsed into laughter at the vision we must have presented.

"As if anyone in their right mind wouldn't recognize us!" Connie said looking in the mirror.

She was right, we looked ridiculous, but nonetheless, it seemed to work and we were settled into our condo for the day.

With several unstructured hours ahead of us, we decided to do what came naturally.

We took naps.

CHAPTER 15

The power nap followed by an early dinner was just what we needed to recharge our batteries for the evening.

While we were napping, Nora gave Devlin his marching orders and he went out searching for Eli. He wasn't answering his cell phone, but with a little sleuthing from Lex, he managed to find him hiding in a small shack deep in the woods.

Shortly before we were ready to go to the rally, my phone rang. Devlin was checking in.

"He thinks you're dead," Devlin said. "He kept asking me if I was sure no bodies were found, especially around the lighthouse. And he kept saying that he heard the banshee like it was a guarantee."

"Okay, that's good to know," Connie said. "Anything else?"

"Yeah, I told him about the rally and that Nora was the one organizing it. As soon as I said that, he immediately forgot about you gals, and what might or might not have happened to you. Instead, he was thrilled that not only was he getting support from his constituents, but that Nora was in charge."

"Good. That's part of the plan. To distract him," I said.

"Well, he's convinced she wants him back, that's for sure. And he's playing games too. Saying he was going to make her sweat a little before he took her back. Said she deserves it. He's a real peach," Devlin muttered.

"Okay, well, be safe, Devlin," I said.

"Sure enough. See you at the rally," he said. "Six o'clock sharp."

After a little debate, and a few more giggles, Connie and I decided, based on our conversation with Devlin, it would be prudent to continue to wear our "excellent" disguises.

A little stressed and very nervous, we met Nora and Clem on the beach. The sun was beginning to set and the shadows were getting longer.

We stayed on the edges of the crowd and tried to be discreet.

"I feel like we're waiting for the guest of honor

at the worst surprise party ever thrown," I whispered to Connie.

As more and more people arrived on the beach we stayed hidden in the shadows, watching quietly. Some knew the real reason they were there, but most believed they were there to support Eli for governor.

"He does have them fooled, doesn't he?" Connie whispered as she pointed to a group who made signs for Governor Alistair.

A six o'clock, Nora took the stage. She stood on a small sturdy table with her back to the water, and she began to speak.

"As you all know, our own Mayor, Eli Alistair, has thrown his hat into the ring and is going to run for governor! Now, Eli and I have had our differences so it might come as a surprise to you that I am endorsing him. But honestly, that only makes me more of an endorsement. Even though we broke up, I still believe in him."

We saw Nora smile as her eyes caught sight of Devlin and Eli at the back of the crowd.

"So far so good," Connie whispered.

"And here is the man of the hour right now!" Nora said. She held out her hand and beckoned Eli to the stage. As Eli strolled through the crowd, Devlin stayed right behind him. He glanced our way and then did a double take. Then he laughed.

I heard him in my mind.

I don't know if you can hear me, if this works both ways. But if you can, you gals are cracking me up with your getups. Those hats are a riot.

I didn't respond.

As Nora stepped down, Eli took the stage. He puffed out his chest and scanned the crowd. As his gaze neared us, we sank into the shadows a little bit more and pulled the brims of our hats lower. Appearing satisfied that whatever he was looking for wasn't there, he smiled smugly and began to speak.

"My good friends and neighbors. I am honored that you are supporting me. We all know I'm the best man for this job. And now, even more people have heard about me. Seems my reputation has gotten out and an official from the party is here tonight. According to him, I am well known even beyond this little place and my popularity is growing. So each one of you should feel proud to say you know me!"

A small ripple ran through the crowd. People were looking at one another and you could tell anger was building.

"Who does he think he is?" Someone whispered.

"I hear some of you grumbling. Let's remember

what happens when people start complaining. Remember those two visitors we had snooping around here? Well, they were complaining about me and now, where are they? You all heard the banshee last night! She wailed twice! Two visitors. See?"

He was talking about us. He truly thought we were dead. And all because we asked questions and snooped around?

"They challenged me. They challenged the way things are here," he said.

"And your family doesn't like to be challenged, does it Eli?" Clem shouted from the crowd. "Any time your family doesn't get things their way, what do they do Eli? Tell the crowd?"

"Oh my goodness! Clem, be careful," Connie muttered to herself.

"I don't know what you mean Clem. It's not my family. It's the banshee. She knows what's best and when she wails, it's for the good of the island. It means she's taking care of business."

"Or is it you?" Clem shouted.

Eli bent down and grabbed Devlin. His mic was still on and we could hear him clearly telling Devlin to get Clem under control.

"Drag him out of here," Eli added.

The crowd gasped again when they heard that and several people surrounded Clem.

Eli climbed down from the table. He ripped the

microphone from his shirt and yelled at Devlin, "Get me out of here. This is all your fault. Why did you bring me here? These people are idiots! Superstitious, insane fools!"

As he climbed down from the table, Nora jumped back up. She spoke in a calm but authoritative voice.

"The banshee doesn't kill. She warns. And she's been warning us about you and your family for generations. We know it all. We've seen the scroll. You are the great great grandson of Silas Hawking!"

Eli stopped and turned.

"How could you possibly have found that out?" He hissed.

"You told us, remember?" I said, as Connie and I dramatically removed our hats.

"Witches!" He screamed. "I killed you! I killed you both on top of the lighthouse. Just like I killed Mildred Raskin and Carson Stewart. Like I killed them all! I'm in charge here. I'm the one with power."

Without hesitation, he grabbed Nora's arm and dragged her off the table. He held her around the neck and a gun suddenly appeared. He must have been hiding it under his shirt.

The crowd was closing in on him by now but backed away when he pointed the gun at Nora's head.

"I'm leaving, and Nora is coming with me."

As he began to drag her down the beach we helplessly followed at a distance. We could hear him muttering to her about living in the woods in the shack.

"You'll be my wife. You'll serve me. I deserve this. I have the power."

Nora continued to fight with every step and we could hear a long string of profanity along with Eli's muttering. She called him every name in the book.

"I've called the sheriff but it'll take him a few minutes to get here," Clem was breathless trying to keep up. "Please don't lose sight of her."

Lex's voice rang in my head.

What do I do?

I told him to keep Nora in sight but to stay hidden and follow them.

Tell me where they end up Lex. Be safe!

Before I had a chance to let Connie know that Lex was with Nora, the banshee let out a blood curdling, long wail that made my knees go weak.

The crowd on the beach stopped and stared. It seemed this was the first time any of them were actually seeing the banshee. What began as an ethereal mist with luminescent colors that swirled in the space just above the water slowly morphed. As the image of her face became visible, we could see that the mist was her hair shimmering in a silver cascade across the water. Her mouth that had produced the mournful wail was now producing a gentle breeze. She was mesmerizing and everyone froze for a split second, taking in her beauty.

Everyone except Eli. "Shut up!" He screamed.

"Let me go, and she will stop," Nora said.

The banshee wailed again and Eli flung Nora to the ground and turned to face her.

"SHUT UP! You do what I command."

"No one commands the banshee."

The ghost of Captain Elias Thorne, large and forbidding, floated in front of Eli. His coat tails billowed behind him as his white hair whipped in the wind that began to pick up. His eyes were black as coal and firmly fixed on Eli Alistair.

"You will leave her alone," the Captain said in a booming voice that made my insides quake.

"What the hell is this?" Eli asked. "Is this a joke?"

He looked frantically from one person to the next.

"Do you people not see this? What is it? A projection or something?"

He began backing away, holding one hand up in front of his face. It was obvious he didn't believe the Captain was a projection and he was becoming more frightened by the second.

"So, what? It's a freaking ghost. And I'm the one you're afraid of?"

"They have nothing to fear from me," the Captain said. Then he looked at Nora. "Go to your friends. You're safe."

The banshee was watching closely and as she pursed her lips, the wind and waves picked up more and more.

As Nora stood, Eli made as though he was going to stop her. He didn't get very far. The Captain moved in a flash and stood between them.

As we gathered Nora into our arms, we could see the Captain had his stone out. It was glowing an eerie green color and causing Eli to back away. He looked frantically in both directions and began running full speed towards the crowd.

Instinctively everyone backed up until someone yelled, "Don't let him get away!"

"Sam, look," Connie nudged me and pointed down.

My pocket was also glowing. I knew what to do.

"Not so fast." I held out my own stone and stood between Eli and the rest of the crowd. The Captain and I began walking closer together and within no time, Eli stood in the lake up to his knees. The waves continued to grow stronger and higher and Eli lost his balance several times.

Still, he continued to scream orders and demands.

"You have no idea what you're messing around with. You people will pay. I'll make sure of it. I deserve it!" He pointed and spat as the waves grew stronger and stronger around. The banshee continued to hover above the water, her lips gently pursed.

"Oh, you'll get what you deserve," the Captain said. "There will be no more tragedy for these people at your hands or the hands of your family. This ends now."

"You'll all go to jail!" The banshee's wail drowned out the sound of his threats.

Nora stepped forward. She turned her face towards the sky.

"Thank you," she said simply.

The banshee's form rippled like a flag in a gentle wind.

"Goodbye, darling," the Captain said. "I am so grateful I got to meet you, my child."

"Goodbye."

"Wait! What's happening? Nora, come out here and save me!" Eli's words faded away as the Captain swooped across the water, snatching Eli up in one arm and carried him, across the top of the lake.

In the distance, something bright yellow

appeared to rise from the middle of the lake. Nora gasped.

"What is it?" Devlin asked.

"Watch," I said.

Soon the body of a majestic ship shot from the depths of the lake and settled on the horizon. We'd lost sight of the Captain and Eli, but we knew Captain Elias Thorne was once again at the helm of the Mystic Mariner.

As the ship turned and began to sail away, we heard his voice boom across the quiet lake.

"Throw him in the brig, men."

The banshee followed behind the ship until the Mystic Mariner was in safe depths. Then both ship and banshee faded away.

CHAPTER 16

"Did you hear?" Connie asked.

We'd been back home now for a week and every day there was new information about the deadly political rally that occurred in a small town along the shores of Lake Huron. As the news spread, investigators flocked to the lighthouse for the story.

"Something new?" I asked.

"Yup," Connie summarized the article. "They are officially stating that an up and coming candidate for governor, and the town's Mayor Eli Thorne, is no longer missing but is now presumed dead when the boat he was on sank in Lake Huron. Rescue crews are continuing to search, but so far neither the body nor the wreckage have been recovered."

"Well, I guess technically that's true," Lex remarked.

"What do you think actually happened to him?" I asked.

"Do you really want to know?" Connie asked. "Or just not think about it."

"Just not think about it," I said. "It gives me the creeps."

"I'm betting it's a *Pirates of the Caribbean* and the Davey Jones thing. Like he's part of the ship now."

"Well, if that's the case, he got what he deserves," Connie said. "Oh, look! This mentions Nora!"

"What does it say?" Lex asked.

"It says Nora Dickson, the town's historian received a large donation for the refurbishment of the lighthouse. They also plan to build another museum next to it to house all the artifacts that were previously kept in a smaller building inland. There will be a brunch at the lighthouse to celebrate the renovations and all the people involved."

"That's amazing! She'll be able to display everything now and tell the entire story. I'm so glad she's getting a happy ending."

"We have to go," Lex said.

Connie nodded. "Agree with you both." She continued to skim the report then said, "Oh, that's perfect."

She covered her mouth as a single tear slipped down her cheek.

"What?" I asked.

"Nothing," she said. "Well, it says here that at the brunch, they are commemorating Captain Elias Thorne and that they will honor him with what was believed to be his favorite drink, Bloody Marys."

This isn't the end for Connie and Sam, but they are taking a little break! While you wait to see what's next for them, check out my new series *Haunted Histories paranormal cozy mysteries!*

If you enjoyed this book, please consider leaving a review or star rating. It's one of the best ways to support independent authors and it lets others know if they might also enjoy this book.

I'd love to stay in touch! **Click here or scan to join my monthly newsletter for updates, sneak peeks, and specials! Paperback, scan the QR code on the next page!**

Find more books by Lynn M. Stout and other cozy mystery authors at the independent book store dedicated to cozy mystery readers! **Visit Mystic Valley Press by scanning the code above.**